Lion on Fire

A CASINO-HEIST THRILLER

Ted Galdi

ISBN: 0989850706

ISBN: 9780989850704

Lion on Fire

One

Stolen diamonds, forged documents, guns. Anything could be in this duffel bag next to me.

A semi-truck honks as I cut it off. Racing across I-80 in New Jersey, I peek at the clock on the console. 5:31 PM. I give my limo some gas, ratcheting it up to eighty-five miles per hour. Only twenty-nine minutes left and I'm not even in the right fucking state.

I weave into the center of the highway, whiz by a Range Rover, then whip back into the fast lane. Damp in a cold sweat, I look at the black bag on the passenger's seat, jostling a bit from my herky-jerky wheelwork.

My boss called me an hour and a half ago. Told me to pick this bag up from a safety deposit box in Jersey. Not open it and not ask questions. Then hand to him in Queens by six PM. A harrowing challenge, from NJ to NY in the belly of a devilish rush hour, without getting pulled over, with the twenty-plus-foot ass of a stretch limo slowing me down and drawing attention to me at the same time.

I gaze at the George Washington Bridge on the horizon. I'm getting close. Then my heart drops as the sea of traffic by the entrance spews into view. I tighten my grip on the steering wheel, sit up in my seat, and muscle my way through the waves of cars, hopping lanes, nosing in front of bumpers, pissing off the surrounding drivers. A hash of horns honks behind me.

5:42 PM. I roll through the toll, the Hudson River and Manhattan's skyline stretching out in my periphery. On open patches of road I speed past other vehicles. In traffic I cut them off. I'm a good driver. Probably the best at my company. Since I got my certification, right after graduating college in May, I've been doing it full-time. But this gig today isn't part of the job description. It's part of a secret I've caught hints of since working at Big Hitter Limousine. One alluded to by whispers, and silence whenever a non-initiate like me got too close.

Though a bit curious, I didn't care enough to pry. I drove my normal shifts and received my normal paycheck. Life was fine. Until last Thursday. When my younger brother told me what he did. And what's going to happen to him unless someone helps.

So I broke the silence. I spoke to Dusty, the company's most popular driver among both employees and clients. If anyone would know the big secret, it'd be him. I asked, hoping what I found out could keep my kid brother safe. Dusty said he could help. And now I'm here, on this lunatic errand for the boss, slicing right toward the Whitestone Bridge exit.

Going fifteen miles per hour over the speed limit, I zip into the rough neighborhood Big Hitter Limousine is headquartered. 5:57 PM, three more minutes. I bang a hard right at the ninety-nine-cent store and turn ninety degrees with a screech. My black stretch zooms by the closed shops on our block, metal gates blasted in spray paint over them. Three punk teenagers on the corner, their hands buried in the pockets of their puffy jackets, watch me sail past with bloodshot eyes.

I pilot the large vehicle into a spot in our parking lot, pick up the duffel bag from the passenger seat, and pelt toward the back entrance of the garage. I go in, my sneaker soles slapping the little gas-puddle islands on the concrete floor. One of the mechanics removes his protective goggles while drilling a hubcap, and says to me, "Whoaaa, easy amigo."

Ignoring him, I keep moving, finally pushing open the brown door in the back corner labeled "Manager."

"I got it," I announce, almost out of time and all out of breath. Panting, I hold up the duffel bag. Barney, my boss, sits behind his desk. Smirking. A few moments pass. No words from him, no movement. Just that damn smirk.

Since he made it clear how stone-written the six-PM deadline was, I figured he'd hop right up, take the bag, and be on his way to putting to use whatever the hell is inside.

"Shut the door," he tells me, in that extra-scratchy voice of his, charred by thousands of packs of cigarettes consumed over the sixty or so years he's been on this planet. I obey and close it.

Standing, he opens his desk drawer. And roots around in it for a while, its contents clicking and clacking. He pulls something out shaped like a pickle. I can't tell what it is from across the room. Tucking it in his back pocket, he struts toward me, stopping about a foot away.

Barney is only about five five, and at five nine I have a view of the top of his head, the ceiling light shining through his thinning red hair, reflecting against the pale skin of his scalp. Despite his size, the guy scares me. Always has.

I've never seen him do anything violent, nor even speak of it, yet he has a sort of intimidating emanation that survives unspoken and undone, that of a man who grew up overly poor and under-educated in Queens and wielded nothing but his street smarts to amass a mini empire of mid-sized, outer-borough businesses, the sort of man who must've done favors for a handful of shady operators on his way up the ladder and may still hold uncashed ones from them.

"I like you, Brian," he tells me.

"Thank you, sir. I like you too."

"But liking someone only means so much. Trusting someone…now, *that*, that means much more."

I'm not sure how to answer, however his eyes are locked on mine and I feel pressure to reply in some way. Before I can muster a thought, he commands, "Let me see the bag."

I hand him it. Gripping it with one hand, he reaches into his back pocket with the other and retrieves the object he removed from his desk. Up close I see what it is.

A knife.

On the wood-grain handle is a red-white-and-blue image of a bald eagle, along with a silver button. He presses the button with his thumb and the blade breaks free from the handle, glinting, like his scalp, in the light above. The sight of the weapon, paired with my confusion in this situation, induces a panic in me, which I try very hard to conceal.

Barney stabs the duffel bag with the knife a couple inches right of the zipper, then digs it in again, his whole arm now buried inside, the black fabric slashed along the bottom.

What the hell is he doing?

Out of the sack floats the sports section of the *New York Post*. Then the business page. Then fashion. Followed by a hard plummet of two cans of Coke.

No diamonds. No documents. No guns.

It was stuffed with newspaper and soda this whole time.

Barney butterflies apart the bag, letting the rest of the newsprint fall to the carpet, then holds the cut-up black fabric to the light and studies it. He's peering inside, at something on the underside of the zipper track. After a few moments, his inspecting expression loosens into one of ease and a smile sweeps across his face. Looking up at me, he says, "Congratulations, you passed."

"I passed what?"

He carries the shredded bag to his desk, sits, and smirks. "Have a seat." He gestures at a chair opposite him.

I sit on the edge of it. "Wait, Barney. I passed *what*?"

He twists the duffel bag inside out, exposing a blue thread tied to the base of the zipper grip at one end and duct-taped to the interior wall of the bag at the other. "A test. The string on the zipper isn't broken," he says.

"Doesn't seem to be," I reply in a slight voice, unaware of what he's getting at.

"That means you didn't try to unzip the bag." He tosses the slashed sack into the trash. "If you gave most people full access to a bag like that, they'd try to open it. Think about taking whatever might be inside for themselves. But not you." He lights a cigarette. "Let me ask you a question. Is there gambling in New York City?"

"No. It's illegal."

He laughs, lightly. "Wrong and right," he says, setting down his gold Zippo. "They don't allow it. But people still do it. You ever hear of the Mayfair Club?"

"Sounds familiar, but I'm not exactly sure—"

"Did you see the movie *Rounders*?"

"With Matt Damon?"

"The Chesterfield Club in *Rounders* is based on the Mayfair Club. It used to be a secret. I played there all the time. The thing with the Mayfair...and this is going back years now, before you were even born...the cops *knew* about it, but looked the other way because...hey, what were we really doing? What were we doing back then that was worse than what all those pimp scumbags and muggers in Times Square were doing? Nothing. We were playing cards. The employees at the Mayfair even had these little medallions they'd wear around their necks. If a crew tried to come in and rob a game, all they'd need to do was hit a little button on the medallion to alert the NYPD. Not only did the cops know about us, they wanted to *protect* us."

"People would rob you guys while you were playing?" I ask, not sure where he's going with all this.

"In any underground game, there's always a risk of someone hitting it. But back then, when the cops were on our side, the risk was less. Any crew in town with the connections to knock off the Mayfair was smart enough to know the NYPD was just a button click away. It was safe." He rests the cigarette in an ashtray and crosses his arms, the shirt material of his sleeves pulling up, the reddish hair on his wrists popping out. "But then it changed. Rudy Giuliani and his goddamn Quality of Life crime campaign. He shut the Mayfair down. A few other prominent underground dens too." He slaps his hands together four times, signaling *zilch*. "No more."

"New ones never opened?" I ask, still not sure how the hell any of this concerns me.

"A few rooms gained followings. But the cops raided them. And these were real *ambushes*, like you'd see on some drug kingpin. Just for cards. For Texas fucking hold 'em. What the cops didn't take into account was the side effect their newfound aggression for us had. It was well known in Manhattan that the NYPD was not a friend of the poker den. They weren't there to protect the players like they used to back in my day. It wasn't long until crews started acting on this bit of knowledge. A few of the dens that were still standing were robbed at gunpoint. I was at one of them when it went down. Some masked motherfucker had a gat against my temple. Made me drop my Rolex into a backpack."

"Jesus. Were the cops more protective after that?"

"Fuck no. They couldn't care less. So, needless to say, around '07 everyone was afraid to play in a New York room." He hits the Marlboro Red and puffs two jets of smoke out his nostrils. "That is, until a friend of mine decided to re-invent the industry. The underground scene in New York is back. In a whole new way. The best way yet. My buddy has Russian contacts who own some of the biggest penthouses in Manhattan, scooped them up for pennies on the dollar during the recession. He doesn't throw his events at the same address in a row, where he's a sitting duck for the cops. He hosts them at a different apartment every Saturday night. And he doesn't even directly let the guests know the locations. He tells his staff the day before, along with one other person." He points at his chest with his thumb and says, "Me. And I tell some drivers of mine that I trust. And they shuttle the guests there. That's how my friend avoids the cops. And that's how he avoids getting robbed. He's always moving. He's been run-ning the most successful club in the history of the City and it doesn't even have a name. That's how he wants it to be. That's how he *needs* it to be. And it's all built on trust. He trusts me. And I need to trust my drivers. It pays a thousand bucks a night." He grinds out the burning cigarette in the ash-tray. "So Brian, can I trust you?"

Two

The red neon of a Samuel Adams beer sign glows against the dull-gray December air in my hometown, Dingan, New Jersey, a blue-collar dot on the US map, plopped next to Alpine and a parade of other posh, white-collar Bergen County suburbs on one side, and on the other Manhattan, its big-moneyed skyline towering above me and the rest of Dingan my whole life, close enough to see but far enough to hear, smell, taste, or touch, a constant refresher by one of the senses that a glamorous life is out there, and a cruel reminder by the four others that we're not part of it.

I'm parked close enough to the bar to recognize anyone walking in, but far enough not to be recognized myself. I shouldn't have come here. If things go as expected, I'll get angry. And what good would that do me? With all that's been on my mind since I spoke with Barney at Big Hitter yesterday, I need calm. I have a lot to think about, and anger clouds thinking a lot.

But I couldn't help it. Now I'm here. So I might as well see this out.

I check the time on my phone. 5:08 PM. Happy hour is underway. It shouldn't be much longer.

Money is tight. And gas is expensive. I keep the engine off, which keeps the heat off, which keeps me freezing in the twenty-something-degree weather. A crystal-crusted chill consumes the windshield glass. I slide my jacket's zipper to its peak, its plastic body lodged against my Adam's apple.

Ten minutes go by, the cold burrowing a few millimeters deeper into my flesh with each passing one. Then, sure enough, there he is.

The onrush of anger heats my freezing skin and I imagine steam wafting off my body in a hot-cold clash, like the pouring of boiling water on a sheet of ice.

My younger brother Kip waltzes along the sidewalk toward Winnie's Pub, no coat, his wire-thin arms protruding from his tee shirt into the front pockets of his baggy jeans, his hands balled under the denim.

Our dad's worked as a Jersey state trooper his entire adult life to put us through college. I went to a four-year state school, and Kip, who didn't nearly have the grades for that, is enrolled in his first year of community college, where he's supposed to be right now, at a sociology course called Individuals and States. Both of us live under the same modestly sized roof with our parents, and I, helping Kip almost every night with his homework, am aware of his entire academic schedule.

For a few minutes I debate what to say to the little shit, then climb out of my Hyundai Sonata and march toward the bar's front door, which looks like a piece of sheet metal, a fragment of the day-drinking crowd coming into view through its diamond-shaped window.

When I push open the door, the saloon stench whacks me in the face, a woody, tinny, sweaty concoction of floorboards wet with fifty years of spilt beer, fixtures barely wet with any soap over the same time period, and the bodies of a dozen or so professional alcoholics perspiring out the chemical byproducts of low-shelf booze and high-calorie food.

Most of them watch Kip, who hasn't noticed me, with friendliness and familiarity on their faces. My nineteen-year-old, fake-ID-toting brother is a regular here. He sticks to his shtick as a liar by entertaining the patrons with a story about him wrestling an alligator down in Florida. Kip's never been to Florida, something they'd never guess from the level of detail he spouts as his beer-bottle-holding hand swings in front of him gesturing for effect.

My grip clasps the top of his arm and his voice cuts short. This "badass," who apparently puts gators in full nelsons, doesn't turn to me with an expression of confrontation, but one of apprehension. It takes a second for him to relax, when the realization kicks in his brother is standing behind him, not a barfly looking for a midday fight.

"Let's go," I say, nodding toward the door. I begin dragging him before he has a chance to reply.

"It's fine," he yells to the crowd in an upbeat tone. "My brother. He's just messing around. Don't worry about me."

I push open the sheet-metal-like slab and pull Kip to the sidewalk, some beer spurting from the neck of his bottle as his hundred-thirty-pound body finds its footing.

"What the fuck man?" he asks, his voice no longer with the cheery facade he feigned for the crowd.

"Throw the bottle out. You're going to get in trouble for having an open container out here."

Kip huffs. Has another sip, then tosses it on a browning patch of grass out front the bar.

"Not on the ground you schmuck. This is *our* town. You want litter all over it? Come on, there'll be a garbage around back."

Kip huffs again, louder this time, like he used to do when we were kids and our mom would ask us to rake the leaves on the lawn. He plods to the discarded bottle, picks it up, and follows me to the rear of the red, brick building, Dingan's Secaucus-bound train tracks entering sight, which run parallel to power lines and the skeletons of trees deprived of their leaves by the Northeast winter.

We stand side by side, both staring at the train-less tracks, neither talking. Kip flings the beer bottle into a dumpster, which rattles against the contents of three overstuffed Hefty bags.

"I know where you're supposed to be right now," I say.

More silence.

He replies, "I got a lot on my mind. You should know that. After what I told you."

"It's no excuse to blow off class."

Finally making eye contact with me, he wings his arms to the sides of his body as if in surprise, and blurts, "Class? You'd have time for class if you were in the shit I'm in now?"

"I told you I'd help you with that. But still, you shouldn't just blow off—"

"You have eighteen grand for me? If you can help me, give me the eighteen Gs. Then I'll go to friggin' *class*."

He does have a point. In light of the recent events, his day-to-day priorities are much different now. So are mine. But still, some nebulous sense of duty inside me, which I don't fully understand, forced me to drive out here and give him crap about ditching school.

It's funny I'm pushing him so hard about college. I went to college and it was far from what I expected. When we were growing up, our parents, neither graduates, made it seem like a degree would be a magic wand in adulthood. I now realize it's more like a timeworn card trick. Sure, it's kind of impressive, but nobody cares all that much. So many people have diplomas nowadays that not having one is a major *disadvantage*, while having one isn't a major *advantage*.

Unless you went to some Ivy League school, and can maneuver your way into a fancy entry-level position in one of those Manhattan skyscrapers on the horizon, recent graduates like me are mostly lost, wandering the streets in search of the shiny door of the illustrious career our parents promised us.

We had a senior-year job fair on my campus. I spoke with some corporate reps who liked me, but their offers were glorified internships, grunt work for twenty-something thousand bucks a year. Sure, I could've advanced over time, but I didn't want to live in my parents' basement or some dinky apartment with three roommates for the better part of my twenties.

I wanted to make money *now*. Save up. Rent my own place by the spring. I drove Uber part-time in college, was good at it, and socked away a consistent flow of spending money. I figured I'd ratchet it up a notch after graduating, so got my New York limo license. The cash isn't spectacular, but I estimate enough to get me out of the nest by April.

So, I don't have much of a right to be pissed at Kip for squandering his college education. Hell, I haven't done anything with mine. You don't need a degree to drive a limo.

I think about this as we watch a train barrel by with metallic rumbles, squeaks, and bangs.

Maybe I care because I believe so much in the rules. I followed the common wisdom of my parents, teachers, coaches, and guidance counselors. I stayed out of trouble. Studied. Got decent grades. Played a couple sports. Did some volunteer work at a local old folks' home. Even joined the debate team because they said it'd look good on my resume.

And no, the college acceptance and eventual degree all this stuff culminated in is no magic wand in my twenty-two-year-old hands. But it has to lead to something someday. I won't drive a limo forever. Yet, while I do, if I keep saving money, keep staying out of trouble, keep shaking peoples' hands and smiling and networking, keep following the rules of society, a bright opportunity will eventually find me. And my life will hit its stride.

That's just how it works. It's worked that way for nearly everyone who's a success today. And it'll work that way for me. And for Kip. If we just play the game.

"I want to help, but I don't have eighteen grand just sitting under my bed," I tell him. "I still don't know why you can't just ask dad. He's not rich, but I'm sure he can scrap that together if he dipped into his retirement money."

"Dad? The judgmental cop? He'd disown me if I told him what I did. He has no clue. No fucking clue, Brian."

I didn't have a clue, either. When I was in college, and Kip high school, he apparently sold weed. This escalated, eventually turning to coke, which he slung to rich kids all over Bergen County this summer. I felt naive when he told me. By then I was done with school and we were living in the same house. The kid hid it well.

Last week Kip picked up a kilo of snow from his connect, a gangbanger in Patterson. It was only the second time he trusted Kip with that quantity. Kip had apparently sold his first kilo quickly, netting a solid profit. After he collected the second, his spirits soaring in expectation of another big take-away, he decided to celebrate.

Kip scooped up his best friend, this wannabe emo musician from Dingan, and treated them both to three hours of private-room lap dances at a strip club in Lodi. When they were done, and giddily strolled back to Kip's car, they noticed the window was broken and the kilo of coke, which my intellectually challenged brother had sitting on the backseat, was gone.

Now Kip's connect, the hoodlum in Patterson, wants the money he would've made if the drugs were sold. Thirty grand. Kip, who had twelve K stowed away from his run as a dealer, ponied up all he had. But he's still eighteen short. Which is why he came to me, his above-board-employed brother.

Kip was given sixty days to pay. There was no way I could generate that sort of money on that sort of schedule on my normal salary, which is why I looked into those whispers of side work that floated around my limo company.

I didn't tell my brother I did that. He has no idea what Barney told me, about the underground gambling ring and my potential to clear a grand a night driving for it. If I mentioned it to Kip, he'd beg I did it. My brother, our family's very own drug dealer, obviously would have no qualms about me breaking the law.

But I would.

"Dad will be pissed if you ask him for help," I say. "*Really* fucking pissed. He might not talk to you for a year. But if this guy in Patterson. This…what's his name?"

"De'Anthony."

"If this De'Anthony is going to rough you up if you don't have the money, dad will bail you out."

Kip holds his gaze on me for about five seconds. A smirk blooms on his face. A chuckle looses from his mouth. "Nobody's roughing me up, Brian. You didn't get that when I told you how much trouble I was in? De'Anthony and his crew will kill me. That's how that world works. You short them on money, you get killed."

The faraway clatter of an approaching train slowly builds. I assumed they'd kick the shit out of him. Break a leg, maybe. Bad stuff.

But kill him?

A spider web of anxiety entangles my guts. My voice speeding up, I say, "If your life is on the line, just ask dad for Chrissake. Who cares if he's mad at you? Who cares if he doesn't talk to you in *ten* years?"

The approaching train is here, a cylindrical haze buzzing past us, the thinner branches of the track-lining bare trees quivering from the rush of motion.

"Of course I considered asking him," Kip says. "Yeah, he'd give me the money. And he probably would talk to me again. Eventually. But you know what I'd be to him? A fuck-up. The same thing he secretly thought I'd turn into my entire life. Him and everyone else. I'm not like you, Brian. You're smart. You'll do something, someday. I don't know what. Something. After what happened, after I left the package on the seat of my car like the goddamn idiot I am, after it got jacked, after all this heat fell on me, I realized I don't want a life like that. I want to be like you. Yeah, I blew off school today. I'm not thinking about class or nothing else until we get this straightened out. I wanted a drink today. I needed to clear my head. But once this is all done, once I come out on the other side...*if* I come out on the other side...I'll do things different. I don't want to be a fuck-up, Brian."

In my brother's face, the same face that's acted its way through so many lies since we were children, is something genuine. And I believe him.

Under all the insecurity and showiness is a good kid. Not the brightest kid. But a good one. He deserves a chance at the game. This is America. We all deserve a chance. Kip's right. If our hard-ass father finds out what my brother did, and he's officially branded a fuck-up at nineteen, and has to live in the same house as a man who thinks he's a waste of his own semen, any confidence he has in himself will erode, as will his shot at any semblance of success.

"I got a job," Kip says. "Night shift a few days a week cleaning up popcorn and shit at the movie theater at the mall."

"You did?" I ask, pleasantly surprised.

"Hopefully it'll help some. Make a dent in the debt." He wipes his runny nose with the back of his wrist. "But no tax-payin', minimum-wage job is covering the whole thing. Not in no sixty days." He glances upward, in thought. "Fifty-four. Now."

With the cash he's bringing in, plus any money I make that I don't need for absolute necessities, plus my scant savings, we can knock out a decent chunk of the eighteen Gs in fifty-four days, but not the whole thing.

Unless, of course, I accept the illegal-casino side gig.

Something just doesn't feel right about it. Kip got into this mess by selling drugs, by veering into the underworld. And now I, the good brother who never broke a rule in his life, am supposed to veer into the underworld myself to get him out of the mess?

It doesn't make sense, like fighting darkness with more darkness.

But what are my other options? Let De'Anthony physically kill him? Force him to crawl to my father for aid, letting the taint of the incident slowly seep into his veins like a poison until he's killed emotionally?

No. I can't let either happen.

I grab the knees of my jeans and hunch forward a bit. "I think I have a way to get you the rest of the money," I say.

"What?" he squawks, his eyes widening. "How?"

I'll do this. But there's no way he's knowing what it is. If he's serious about straightening out his life like his big brother after this dilemma is resolved, the image of his big brother as a criminal can only distort and disturb that vision.

"Just trust me," I reply. "Okay?"

He nods, eyes still wide.

"Come on," I say. "Let's go back in there. I need a beer too."

Three

Driving down my street in Dingan, the night-shadowed neighbors' houses beside me, I think about this block and the world it's part of, the one I've been part of my whole life, one where things are tidily and unabashedly connected in plain sight, dutiful citizens to dependable jobs and dependable jobs to the mortgage payments on these dependable homes around me and these homes to solid American lives for solid American children soon to grow into dutiful citizens themselves.

But tonight, for the first time, this isn't my world.

Tonight I'm part of a different one, an underground one that's far from above-board. I told Barney I'd drive the casino job. And tonight is my debut.

I cruise in my Sonata through the asleep suburban streets toward Route 4, which should soon port me into the hubbub of a New York City Saturday night.

The instructions Barney gave me were simple enough, yet anxiety still finds a way to pump through every pore of my body, as if it were permeating from the air vents of the car. I've been a wreck all day. Back at the house, before I left, I was watching the Knicks game on TV with my dad and, so preoccupied about tonight's task, called a free throw an extra point replying to one of his comments.

Anyway, I'm supposed to park at Big Hitter like I would for a normal shift and hop in my limo. At exactly nine PM I'll receive a text from Barney with three pieces of information. My pickup corner. The drop-off location. And the password. I'm to immediately go to the pickup corner, where invitees to the casino will be waiting, whom I'll shuttle to the drop-off address upon their providing of the password, then repeat the steps through the evening.

Secretive and stealthy, Barney's friend who runs the casino has no tolerance for mistakes. I'd lose the privilege of driving for him if I fucked any of this up, even a little.

Which could literally be deadly. Without that extra income, the thousand bucks every Saturday night, Kip will be short on his debt to De'Anthony, resultantly cutting his life short.

I flip on the radio, hoping a little music will relax me. A midway-through "You Don't Mess Around with Jim" by Jim Croce crackles through the worn sound system. Over the next half hour I navigate NJ then NY with one hand on the steering wheel, the other attempting to keep the beat of Q104.3's rock lineup with rhythm-challenged taps and pats on my thigh.

The nerves don't go away.

I decide to distract myself another way. Let's check in on the Knicks, see if they've held the lead they had when I left. I reach to the cup holder, where I usually keep my phone, to scope the score. But it isn't there.

Maybe I left it in my pocket. I check my left-pants one. Then right. My heart swells against my ribcage. It must be in my coat. Nope. Possibly the inside pocket of my suit jacket, the only remaining option.

I inch my hand across my chest, under the black flap of fabric, then slowly dip my fingers through the interior slit, my sense of touch wishfully expecting the familiar hard-rubber feel of my iPhone case.

But it doesn't come.

As they plunge deeper, my fingers contact nothing but the silky, billowy folds of the pocket.

"Fuck," I scream, my head jutting over the steering wheel, spit shrapnel striking the windshield. "You fucking asshole," I call myself. Because I am. Only a fucking asshole would leave his phone back at his house on a night when he needs his phone to receive vital instructions about a job vital to his brother's survival.

I lean back in the seat, sucking a big breath in and sending it out as I attempt to collect myself. Preoccupied, I must've left it on the sofa where I was watching the game with my dad.

Sure, I can go back and get it, but with a glance at the console clock, see it's already 8:46 PM. And I'm already in Queens. If I drive the forty minutes all the way back to Jersey, then the forty all the way back here, I'll have the addresses and password, but arrive extremely late for my first pickup, a definite fuck-up and disqualifier for future casino work.

I'm five minutes from Big Hitter. Hopefully Barney is in the office. If he is, I can ask him for the info in person.

A flash of optimism surges through my chest. But fades once I acknowledge the plan is dependent on Barney sitting around the office late on a Saturday night, something I've never seen him do.

I don't know his number off the top of my head, but maybe I'll cross paths with another driver once I get to headquarters. They could lend me their cell phone to call Barney from.

I take another deep breath as the glow of the Big Hitter sign, written in the font the New York Yankees use, gradually brightens against the foggy winter night as I near it. I park in the back, among the contradictory mishmash of luxury limousines the company owns and mediocre personal vehicles their drivers do.

Dashing toward the garage's back entrance, I pray someone is inside. Anyone, as long as they have Barney's number saved in their phone, which most must. I yank on the door. Locked. An almost-assured signal nobody is here.

I use the company key to open it, and yank the slab toward me. My eyes wildly scanning the garage, my fear is confirmed. Empty.

A thwack booms behind me as gravity swings the door shut, its echo radiating through the vacant space. My stare shoots to Barney's closed office door. Could he be inside? Toiling away on some paperwork? It's a possibility. And my only chance at a recovery.

With footsteps that sound both light with anticipation and heavy with skepticism, I cross the tool-strewn garage surface to the boss's office. I knock. No answer. I turn the knob and enter. No Barney.

Oh, no.

My shoulders deflate as any wishful trace sputters out of my body. I pace the garage for about five minutes, my mind laboring for a solution, locating none.

Then, my drooped shoulders perk up as a familiar sound clangs behind me. The garage door. Its rickety joints and jamb squealing as they did just before, but voiced by the opening of the slab, versus closing. Someone is here. Someone who can most likely help.

I half-twirl toward the noise. And yes, someone is here. And no, I never would've guessed who in a thousand fucking years.

Standing in the Big Hitter garage, the darkness and heaviness of his black moustache brought out by the overhead-lamp-washed paleness of the wall behind him, is my father, still wearing the Russell Athletic sweatpants he had on in the den when we were watching the Knicks, a canvas jacket now up top.

His face emits a special kind of suspicion. Not the traditional fatherly kind that'd come my way as a kid when he thought I didn't study for a test as much as I said I did, but the professional kind, the type I've seen him employ when his police colleagues go over the details of a case with him.

"Hey," is all I can think to say. A pause. "What are you doing here?"

"I thought you said you were meeting up with some college buddies at a bar in Edgewater."

I did say that. When he asked me where I was going when I left during the Knicks game. I told him it was an upscale bar, hence the suit. The last few days, living in the house with him after I consented to illegal side work, has been mentally taxing. He's a state trooper. A damn good one. And he's made a career out of sniffing the illegality out of seemingly legitimate situations. He's got a cultivated sense for it, sort of like how a good chef can take a whiff of a seemingly perfect vegetable and know it just won't taste right in a dish.

So I wanted to keep him as mentally removed from the casino as possible. Mainly, in the event the whole thing blows up one day and Big Hitter is exposed as a conspirator, I could play dumb, saying I never worked Saturday nights and knew nothing about any casino.

That way, my reputation as the "good son," something important to me and imperative to him, would stay intact. He spent his life working hard to raise two boys, furnish them with opportunities he never had, and foster their rise to a better place. One of those kids, though not an evil person, is surely a misfit, saddling me with the brunt of the burden of converting my father's hopes into a worthwhile payoff. If he found out Kip sunk into the underworld he'd be demoralized. If he found out I went with him, he'd be devastated.

But I guess there's no way of hiding I work Saturday nights now. My best bet is to just play this naturally. "I was on my way to the bar," I say, "then got a call from work, wanting me to go in. I had to skip out on my buddies to come here."

"Huh," he says.

Silence.

He reaches into a pocket of his canvas jacket. "How did you get a call from the road if you didn't have a phone?" He removes his hand, revealing my iPhone in his grip.

The sight of it is both jubilant and jarring. My phone is here, which means I can read Barney's message and ride over to my pickup spot. I'm now running late, but likely not late enough to ruin the whole schedule.

What I can't salvage though is the stone-faced lie I just told my dad, which he smacked down like a feather.

He hands me the phone and says, "I noticed it on the couch after you left. Thought you'd want it, so I jumped in my car and followed you, figuring you were only going ten minutes into Edgewater. When I saw you heading another direction, I kept following. Kept going until I got here. Wanted to make sure everything was all right."

He was behind me the whole time. And I had no clue. Another cop skill he's mastered over the years. "Yeah, everything is all right. Just working late is all."

Neither of us speaks, that professional suspicion in his expression seeming to sharpen with each passing second. After about ten, in a throaty yet distant voice, he says, "Good. Good."

But he isn't good. He knows I'm up to something. And without a goodbye, he leaves.

Four

Zipping out of the Big Hitter lot in my Lincoln limo, I peek at my precious phone where, sure enough, a text message from Barney's been waiting. At the top is "1 and E 81, NW corner." Below that, "Omocron Tower. Park and E 71." Finally, at the bottom, "Honeydew."

9:08 PM. Eight minutes behind schedule, which in the world of professional chauffeuring is an eternity. One customer complaint about lateness on my first night can relegate me from high-paid insider back to regular driver.

Not a short trip, a nine-and-a-half-mile shepherd's hook to the Upper East Side via Grand Central Parkway.

I traverse the roads how I did during my duffel-bag test, fast enough to make up for slipping time, just slow enough not to give any cop who doesn't feel like writing a ticket a moral obligation to have to.

Traffic is light. And I'm moving the Lincoln well. Positivity bubbles in my stomach. It looks like this all might work out.

I cross the Robert F. Kennedy Bridge and prepare to merge onto the FDR. Then notice the exit is closed. "Shit," I grumble, remapping an alternate route in my head.

My attention drifts from the actual road to a grid of theoretical ones in my mind. Until a loud pop snaps my focus back to the here and now.

Holy shit, I think I just hit something.

I stop the car and close my eyes. Hoping it wasn't a person. In a few seconds, when I open them, I notice a disheveled man through the windshield. His body is draped in rags, his face dotted in soot, however he doesn't seem injured.

"What the hell you doin'?" the vagrant shouts, gesturing toward an upturned shopping cart in the street, his belongings fanning from it across the pavement, used soda cans and trash bags and odd, one-off items like a lone drumstick.

9:33 PM on the clock. No doubt my first wave of riders is already waiting at the pickup corner, the winter wind creeping under their clothes, aggravation mounting about their late driver.

Who's about to be a lot later. The homeless guy is positioned at the nose of the limo, barring me from driving on.

"Help me clean this shit up," he says.

I don't have time for this. But it was my fault. And I do feel bad. Everything he owns is disarrayed across the street. Not to mention, with him blocking me, I don't have a choice.

So I flip the hazards on and shut the engine off. As I climb out of the limo, the fumy air, tinged with exhaust from recently passed vehicles, clogs my nostrils and mouth. Coughing, I scuttle to his slew of stuff. Gathering a semi-crushed Sprite can, I realize this was my first traffic accident ever.

I'm just not right tonight. First the phone. Now this. I'm not cut out for the illicit, this entire casino thing scrambling my mind. As much as I hate it, I tell myself I have to go through with it. The sanctity of my little brother's life outweighs that of my mental health.

Over the next ten minutes or so, with me behind a good eighty percent of the work, every can, bag, miscellaneous knickknack, and even scattered piece of change is tucked back into its proper place, as dictated by the owner.

"You're all set," I say.

He eyeballs the full, upright cart.

"Have a good night," I tell him, backpedaling toward the limo. As a so-long, he spits on the pavement, a foot or so in front of my feet, then roams to the cart and begins pushing it to God knows where.

I resettle behind the wheel and return to my re-route. Afraid of what it'll tell me, I don't even look at the clock. I hustle through traffic, bombing through a light a moment after it turns red from yellow, eliciting two angry honks from the intersection.

Soon I slam to a stop at the northwest corner of 1st Avenue and East 81st Street. The gazes of eight well-dressed men, each holding a briefcase, rush to my limo. The most irritated-looking one is a Wall Street type with the beginnings of an old man's turkey neck but wrinkleless cheeks and forehead, as if he recently got a facelift and doesn't go back for the neck job for another few weeks. He approaches my vehicle, signaling for a window roll-down.

I comply and say, "Good evening."

He greets me with only a scowl. Then asks, "Do you happen to know where my acquaintances and I can find any honeydew in this neighborhood?"

Honeydew. The password. "I know just the place," I tell him. I get out and open the door for them, realizing how badly

I have to piss upon standing and moving around. I took down two Dr. Peppers during that Knicks game back in Jersey.

As the others funnel into the limo, their turkey-necked speaker lingers behind, still scowling at me. Once the rest are inside, he says, "You were late," holds the glower for another couple seconds, then enters.

Christ. This asshole is going to complain about me. He's probably used to perfection, a managing director at one of the megabanks who has a hundred doting employees. I try not to think about it, focusing on the task at hand, getting this crew over to the location.

I do, then zip back to my corner, my bladder ballooning. To avoid any further time loss, I keep the piss trapped inside me, not stopping for a bathroom break as I bang out pickups and drop-offs on repeat.

This goes on for over two hours, ending at midnight, which is what Barney instructed. The drivers are allowed to hang out at the event once we're done with our part. *Allowed* is actually the wrong word, *required* more like it. A security measure. Barney's friend in charge doesn't want us wandering the city with the address in our heads while the function is going on, in case we slip up and mention it to the wrong person. So to keep us contained we get to come.

I park the limo in a nearby garage, then trudge along the sidewalk, my pent-up bladder pulling on all the muscles in my abdomen with each step. I look around for a place I can take a leak, a restaurant, a bar, a store, anything, but all I see are rows of cars and canopies of residential buildings.

Though I had a rocky start tonight things seemed to work out in general, except for that one jerk with the turkey neck. The image of those droopy-skin folds hangs in my head like a pebble in a shoe, a reminder that he's currently at the event, likely to complain about me and cancel this critical income stream for me.

I finally make it to the building, Omocron Tower, my pelvis quivering from all the piss locked behind it. A doorman lets me in and I survey the plush lobby for a toilet sign. A painting of the French Riviera. A tan couch with a country-club feel. An oak-paneled desk. No bathroom. No relief.

I provide my name at the desk, then take the elevator up to the penthouse. The doors don't open to a hallway but right inside the place, the marble floor glossy and white like the pearls of some royal. Blocking most of my view is a six-foot-six guy who looks like a Soviet commando, the outline of his muscles swelling beneath his black blazer and turtleneck.

"Password?" he asks.

"Honeydew."

With a bear-paw hand, he signals for me to enter.

"Thanks," I say, stepping inside. I take in the unobstructed view, a Baby Grand piano on my left, behind it an imperial staircase with mahogany banisters, and above me a chandelier with a pinkish-gold sheen, its flower-petal-shaped lamps gleaming down on the foyer's artwork, a diamond-encrusted bust, a crystal sculpture, a vase of a pagan god.

To my right, voices, music. I walk across the marble toward the noise, under an archway and on to the sight in the next room. The ceiling jumps from ten feet to twenty, the floor widening under a crowd of around eighty, two craps, black-jack, and roulette tables, six poker ones, a seven-piece band on a stage, and gorgeous cocktail waitresses circulating amid it all.

This sure as hell is no underground casino. This is about as high up as you can get, the tallest floor of one of the tallest residential buildings in New York, done up in high-flying Park Avenue style. For privacy the curtains are drawn on all the windows, but if they were open we'd be floating over Manhattan.

As the band's trombone contends with the wailing sax I wander deeper into the crowd, swiveling my head, soaking up the scene.

Off the main room is a study appearing to have been converted into the cashier station for the night. A man removes a wad of bills from his briefcase and hands them to an older lady at a desk, who puts them through an automated counting machine, the kind they have at the bank, then reaches to a colorful rack of chips and picks him off three stacks, all while a security guard the same size as the one by the elevator scrutinizes every aspect of the exchange. The attendee passes the lady his briefcase, then she puts a tag around the handle and hands him a claim ticket, just like you'd see at a coat check.

Glancing at the faces in the crowd, I spot a few other Big Hitter employees, each drinking water as opposed to booze like the rest, drivers of course not allowed to drink at these events.

Speaking of company employees, I wonder where Dusty is, the guy I came to when I first inquired about side work. He vouched for me, convincing Barney to give me the duffel-bag test, and is effectively responsible for this opportunity to earn essential cash.

So enthralled by the glamor of this casino, I almost forgot how badly I have to piss. I ask someone where the bathroom is and he points me toward the foyer, saying it's directly on the other side. As I meander there through the attendees, chatter at the tables buzzes by my ears. "No field five, no field five." "Double down." "Red nineteen."

The singer in the band, a black guy in his fifties with a fedora, sunglasses, and rose pinned to his lapel, is belting out "Jump in the Line" by Harry Belafonte. "And fellas you got to watch it, when she wind up, she bottom, she go like a rocket..."

I cut through the gyrating group on the dance floor and cross back into the foyer. Above me I hear footsteps and the jingle of bangles. A striking figure descends the stair-case, a view I stop to watch. A girl, early twenties, button nose, blond hair, the same sequin top and short skirt the cocktail waitresses have on. However, unlike the others, her legs lack fishnet stockings. She catches me staring at her. I, who's never been particularly smooth with females, awk-wardly take out my phone and pretend to text someone.

She reaches the bottom of the steps and scoots toward the main room, her high heels tapping against the marble, and I progress with my trip to the bathroom. A few strides in, another figure on the staircase grabs my attention. It's Dusty.

On his body are the elements of the official driver uniform, black suit, tie, and white shirt, yet worn non-uniformly, the sleeves of the jacket rolled up to mid-forearm, tie swinging from his neck loose-knotted, shirt untucked. He runs a hand through his wild, dirty-blond hair, and begins climbing down the steps.

On his face is a mischievous expression, a gentle bite on the lower lip, a subtle twinkle in the blue eyes. His cheeks are a bit rosy, as if he's been performing some physical activity. Then it hits me.

He was upstairs screwing that waitress.

I let out a light gasp. My head swings in the direction she went, then settles back on him. Noticing me, he grins. He knows I know. His mischievous expression transforms into one of the opposite nature, innocence, the lips pursed in and eyebrows popped up, as if to say, *Don't blame me, she was beautiful, what was I supposed to do?* I shake my head and laugh.

"Bri," he says, greeting me with a smack on the shoulder.

"You're unbelievable," I say.

He shrugs, modestly, then pulls a flask from his jacket pocket. He takes a sip and extends it to me.

"What the hell are you doing?" I ask.

With the back of his hand, he wipes his lips, then says, "It's not like they're breathalyzing us on the way out." He rattles the flask a couple times.

"I can't."

"Suit yourself." He has another gulp, then stows it in his jacket pocket. "C'mon," he says, striding toward the main room while tucking his shirt back in. "I've got someone I want you to meet." I follow him through the archway, back into the action.

Dusty leads the way through the crowd, people going out of their way to say hi to him about every five seconds.

He brings me to a broad-shouldered, late-forties man in a flashy suit who's engaged in conversation with a raven-haired female guest. "Pardon me," Dusty says, politely interrupting their chat. "Igor, you have to meet someone." He nods at me. "This is Brian, our newest driver."

The man raises a finger to the woman, indicating for her to give him a minute, then turns to me and smiles. He's handsome in a friendly way, like the sort of actors in toothpaste commercials. "Brian, good to meet you," he says, his voice specked with a Russian accent, as if he were born there but living in America for a while. "I'm Igor."

"Good to meet you too," I say.

While we shake hands, Dusty adds, "This is Igor's operation. He runs the show."

"It's a heck of a show," I say, gesturing to the elaborate surroundings.

"Ah," Igor replies, "I have a great staff. All the credit goes to them. Enjoy yourself. If you need anything at all, just ask for me."

"Will do. Thanks."

He gives me a thumbs-up, then returns to his convo with the lady.

Dusty motions for me to follow him, but before he has a moment to move a man breaks off from the mass and says to him, "Dusty, was looking for you, wanted to say what's up." A bit on the shorter side, he has a crown of neatly combed white hair on his head and a warm, drunk smile on his face. "Things are good?"

"Can't complain. You look awesome. Lose a little weight?"

"I better have, for the hundred dollars an hour I'm paying that personal trainer at my club."

Dusty chuckles.

"How'd that project turn out?" the guys asks. "The one you were telling me about a couple weeks ago."

Dusty's eyes and smile spark. He pulls out his cell phone, holds up the screen, and says with pride, "All done."

"Looks nice."

"The fluted legs took me a lot of time, with—"

"Wait, the what?"

"The fluted legs. It's a special style of table leg, where evenly spaced, vertical grooves are carved into the wood. Kind of like in Greek columns." Dusty clicks a few buttons on his phone and says, "Here, look at a close-up."

I peek at the screen, on it a photo of a table leg with four narrow valleys. It's professionally done and I can appreciate the craftsmanship, yet it looks like a leg you'd see on a million other pieces of furniture. It's nothing unique to me, and peering at the white-haired man's face, I can tell it's nothing special to him. Yet, to Dusty, who has a woodworking hobby, it's much more.

"A couple years ago, I could only do a standard fluted leg," Dusty tells us. "I'd never be able to do something like this. It's the way the cherry tapers at the bottom. *That's* the tricky part." Though table legs are boring and I don't really care about "the way the cherry tapers," how Dusty talks about all this makes you want to listen. His voice is charged with something as he speaks, something from somewhere deep, somewhere you can't help but want to learn more about.

The other man knows this just as much as me, and to keep the conversation going asks, "So where's the table now?"

"At a little market in Pramin, where I live. When I finish something I don't keep for myself, they let me put it out front to sell."

"Maybe when you do your next one, instead of selling it there, I'll pay you a fair price for it. I can always use some new stuff for my houses. What do you think?"

"Done."

"Great. See you around, Dusty." With a thankful smile, the man strolls toward the poker tables.

As soon as he's gone, someone else approaches Dusty for a little face time. Then someone else. And someone else.

This one I recognize. The turkey neck.

The muscles in my legs clench when I see him. He obviously hasn't told on me for being late yet or else Igor, the organizer, would've mentioned something when I met him.

However, him seeing me now may remind him of my timing imperfection, prompting him to take action.

As he chats with Dusty, his face is free of the scowl it reserved for me. However, it crops back up once he notices me. We stare at each other for a few seconds.

"You two know each other?" Dusty asks.

"He drove me here tonight," the man says, his voice shifting from a friendly to a snooty tone. "He was late."

"Well, you're here now," Dusty coolly says, "and it's a hell of an event. It's Brian's first night. Cut him a little slack if he was a few minutes behind schedule, all right?"

The man keeps his gaze on me a bit longer. And then, and it's subtle, offers a hint of a nod before turning his attention back to Dusty.

I'm saved.

I've been so wrapped up in Dusty's orbit I again forgot to piss. I tell him I'll be back in a bit, then set out toward the bathroom.

He steps onto the dance floor, where a sixtyish woman grabs his hand and starts fox-trotting with him. With a smile he goes along with it, the fat diamonds in her earrings sparkling as they swing around.

I finally make it to the bathroom. And let out what's been bottled up. It feels good. It feels really good.

Five

I slide the front end of the pool stick forward then back along the cradle of skin between my left thumb and index finger, tighten my right hand around its base, then pump it forward, smashing the tip into the cue ball, a barely noticeable poof of blue chalk appearing under the glow of the Rolling Rock lamp above the table as the ball cranks into the triangular arrangement of fifteen others, breaking it into shards of green, red, white, orange, purple, blue, maroon, and black. *Petunk*. I hear one go in but don't see which.

"You got highs," Dusty confirms from the other end of the table, a pool stick in his left hand, a glass of Budweiser in his right. "The ten ball went in here." He smacks a corner pocket with his cue.

We're at Dakota Shirley's, a pub in Pramin Township, the mountain village in upstate New York where Dusty lives, about fifty miles from the city. It's Friday and we both have off, so I asked him if he wanted me to buy him a drink, a thank-you for him hooking me up with the side work at the casino.

I take a shot on the "14" but miss. Dusty rests his beer on the ledge of the table and angles up for the "3" in the corner pocket, his eyes intense. *Petunk*. He chalks his cue, leans over, and takes aim at a complex shot on the "7." *Petunk*.

You'd figure a guy like him would've had plans on a Friday night, the type of guy who made all those people at the gambling event fawn, the type of guy who effortlessly beds beautiful girls. But he was wide open. Not because he couldn't find something else to do, more because he couldn't be bothered to try. As engaging as he may be when he's out in a crowd in Manhattan, from the little I know of him, his natural state is up here, in the quiet of the woods.

He thrives off the city in small doses, but I could never picture his home there. The eternal hustle of Manhattan seems to be a song he has never sung yet already knows the words to at twenty-four, a song with lyrics about the right reservation at the right restaurant on the right night, and the better career, and the richer acquaintances, and the semi-famous friend of a friend you say hi to in front of other guests at a party, and the invitation to that gallery opening you heard the mayor's wife was going to, and the hope to be recognized for something, and the fear you never will. He knows these lyrics and seems bored by them.

But when he's in Pramin, a curiosity roars about him. I can tell already and this is only my second time up here, my first merely days ago when I first spoke to him about the side gig.

I finish the last sip of my beer, then ask him, "Another round?"

He takes a gulp of his, dumping the rest down his throat, then flicks me a thumbs-up. "Let me give you a few bucks."

"Nah, they're on me tonight." Watching him knock in the "1" ball, I ask, "Speaking of money, how much would you say flows through the casino on a given night?"

"A shitload." He tilts forward, nails the "5" in the far corner, then glances up at me. "Why?"

"No reason. Just curious. It must be pretty sizable. Let's try to figure it out. There were about eighty people there. Probably fifty were seriously gambling. What do you think the average bet size was? What frequency of bets would you say the typical player makes in an hour?"

He twists some chalk on his cue. "I don't feel like doing math right now. I thought you were going to get us another beer."

"Fine, fine, no math," I concede, with a chuckle. "It's just interesting to think about how much money Igor has to put up each week to bankroll the house. He must be extremely wealthy. Do you know what line of business he's in?"

"What do you mean?"

"Like for work. How he made all the money to start a casino."

The Rolling Rock lamp illuminates a smirk emerging on Dusty's face. He laughs and asks, "You don't know?"

"How would I know? Did Barney tell you? He didn't tell me."

Still grinning, he walks to the other side of the table and bangs in the "6" ball. "Open your eyes, Brian."

"Open them to what?"

He blows blue chalk residue off the top of his stick. "It's against the law. It's highly organized. It's held in penthouses owned by wealthy Russians..."

"Yeah, so?"

He shakes his head. "Russian mob. Barney got to know a bunch of the big shots over the years."

The jabbering voices of the bar patrons blend into one hazy hum behind me. Russian mafia? For fucking real?

Petunk. In goes the "4 " ball. Dusty whacks the corner pocket with his hand, calling his shot for the "8." As he hunches over, he asks, "You all right over there?" He shoots, putting it in, ending the game, beating me.

His face is composed, his shoulders relaxed, as if we were chatting about sports or the weather. "I'm going to get the beers," I say, needing some space.

The mob. How could I not have put it together? How could I be so naive? A suffocating panic begins accumulating in my chest and I feel like running clear out of here and never looking back on any of it, on Dusty, on Barney, on the casino.

But then the rational, college-educated side of my brain corrals things into perspective.

Kip.

I'm doing this for Kip. I already knew it was illegal, had issues with it, yet walked into the fire to help him. Sure, the revelation that the mafia is involved amplifies the heat, but doesn't afford me an out. I promised my brother I'd have his back. And I'm not backing out of that.

However, I then consider our father, imagining what he'd say if he found out his eldest boy were a mob affiliate. He'd probably say nothing, actually. His soul would just crash into shame-induced cardiac arrest.

The last few days at the house, ever since he surprised me at Big Hitter with my phone, he's been acting strangely. He hasn't mentioned the incident once, or the lie he so clearly caught me telling, however, he's definitely still carrying around something about that night. He knows I'm up to something, but not what in particular. If he did, he'd act on it, accuse me with specifics like he would a perp in an interrogation room.

I tell myself it's Friday night, that I've had an extremely stressful last couple weeks, and need to stop stewing over all this and enjoy myself before I go mad.

So I grab the beers, toss four more quarters into the pool table, and start another game. As Dusty knocks his stick into the cue ball, a stocky male figure bumps into his hip. It's a guy a little older than us shooting pool the next table over, shaved head, zit-infested face, Pantera tee shirt with a flannel on top.

"You good, man?" Dusty politely asks, deeming the bump an accident.

He stares into Dusty's face for a couple seconds, chomping with his jaw as if he were chewing gum. "Yeah man," the guy says. "I'm good."

He goes back to his table, joining his two friends, the smaller one wearing a camouflage tee shirt, and the bigger one looking like a warrior from the Middle Ages, a wiry orange beard wrapping his chin in uneven clumps, a raised scar on his left cheek like an earthworm bound to his skin. The whole trio leers at us.

I've never been to a place like Dakota Shirley's. A dive, but not the type you'd find in Jersey or the city. It's a mountain bar with a rural aura, however, most of the dudes in here don't come off as friendly-farmer types, a lot wearing expressions that seem to suggest a deep state of boredom welcomingly waiting to be snapped by any type of trouble.

"Your shot, Bri," Dusty says. I take it, not only botching the "11" in the close corner, but scratching. As he retrieves the cue ball from its return cubby I glimpse the threesome again to see if they're still watching us. Just the little one with the camouflage shirt, with side eyes, his fake-diamond earring shining in our direction.

I don't want him to catch me staring back so I move my eyes off him and drag them aimlessly around the place, over a Big Buck Hunter arcade machine with an "out of order" sign, a mirror on the wall with an etched Jim Beam logo, the snowy lawn of the closed post office outside the front window. My focus freezes on the bar. Among the mostly male, mostly beastly crowd is a pair of girls, their looks and laughter glowing against the drab surroundings like treasure-chest coins peeking out from the seafloor under a shipwreck.

Dusty notices me scoping them and jokes, "You squaring up for the ten ball, killer, or something else?"

I flip him off, then take a crack at the "10," missing, knocking it into the "4," one of his balls, almost putting it in for him. "Crap," I mumble.

"Eh, eh, eh, one must focus on one thing at a time," he says in a taunting voice, with a taunting smirk, then nods toward the girls. "You know what they say. If you have more than one priority…you have none." He strikes the cue ball, sending it on a long ride across the green, dropping in the "4" I left close for him. He saunters around the table in my direction and says, "They're cute. Which one you going for?"

"It's your shot. Come on and take—"

"Don't bullshit me. I saw you looking. Which one you like?"

I fidget, squishing my sneaker sole against the floor. "The blonde a little better than the brunette," I say softly. "But, Dusty, it's not—"

"Got it. You take the blonde, I'll take the brunette." He gestures toward them with his elbow. "Well, what're you waiting for?"

"What do you mean?"

"You're not going to talk to her?"

"Just go up to her and start talking?"

"As opposed to what, going up to her and backflipping?"

We chuckle. I hope the brief moment of levity interrupts the chain of the discussion and he doesn't keep pressing me about speaking to her, something I'm deathly afraid to do. Unfortunately he doesn't quit, adding, "You get it going with her, then I'll come over and wingman the friend."

"That girl is really hot. She doesn't want to date someone like me. She's probably into older guys. Established guys with money. Not some limo driver in his early twenties."

"I take offense," he says jokingly. "I'm a limo driver in my early twenties too."

In all seriousness, he does have a point. Dusty doesn't have much money or any sort of social status, the two key things I always assumed males needed to attract quality females. Yet women love him, from young cocktail waitresses to golden-years Wall Street heiresses.

It must be because he's good-looking. I'm a six at best. Things are different for handsome guys.

Then again, I've had a handful of handsome friends over the years and none of them had the sort of effect on girls Dusty does. Which makes no sense, given he isn't richer or better connected than any of them.

"I'm not playing pool any longer unless you go up there and talk to her," he says.

I feel my face heating up. "What do I even say? What's my pickup line?"

He shakes his head. "Pickup lines are the dumbest things of all time. With a pickup line you're immediately telling her that you're there for her, some desperate dude willing to do whatever she says in order to get into her pants. But see, girls don't want that. When it comes to hooking up, girls are selfish."

I don't understand this logic, seems flipped. "Wouldn't the first thing be selfish of her though? If I was willing to do whatever *she* wanted, and *she* let me?"

"No, no, no." He presses his back and the bottom of his right boot against the wall. "That's not selfish because a guy like that, a guy willing to do whatever she puts him through, makes her do all the heavy lifting in the…relationship. A guy like that is a work in progress, still needs to be melded and molded. Girls, especially the good ones, they don't want a work in progress. They don't want to do the heavy lifting. They want a guy to come into their life who's already got his own life figured out. He doesn't necessarily *need* them. A guy like this doesn't use a pickup line. He just acts like himself and trusts she'll take notice. With a guy like this, the girl doesn't have to do any work. See. Selfish."

"When you say a guy with his own life figured out, you mean one with money, right? That's what I was trying to tell you before. They want—"

He laughs. "Having your life figured out and having money are two completely different things."

I'm not exactly sure what he means, though the confidence in his expression tells me it makes perfect sense in his own head.

"Fine," I say. "If no pickup line, what do I talk about?"

"It doesn't matter. Anything. As long as you come off as someone who's comfortable in his own skin. There're no tricks to it."

I feel myself falling into that orbit of his, the one that swoops you up and makes you magically forget about your preoccupations. And though my face is a thousand degrees, though my mouth is as dry as ash, I decide to listen to him.

With a big swig, I finish my beer, then firmly set it down on the rim of the pool table. Marching along the wooden floorboards, I approach the girls. My face is so hot it must be visibly red, but I try not to think about it. Stay focused, Brian. Stay cool. Like Dusty said, just come off as comfortable.

I wedge my right rib against the bar, plant my elbow down, and signal "one more" to the bartender. As he pulls on the ice-glacier-shaped Coors Light tap handle to fill a pint glass for me, I peek to my left at the blonde. And realize I have absolutely nothing to say.

My stare scuttles about the place, again passing over that out-of-order Big Buck Hunter video game. And I blurt out to her, "You look familiar. Were you in here the other night when that nut job tried to steal the arcade machine?"

Out of all the things I could've possibly said, I really couldn't tell you why my mind landed on this. It's clearly a lie. I've never been here before, and know nothing about the history of the arcade machine.

The girl-to-girl conversation halts to a scary silence and the blonde looks up at me, her pear-green eyes suspiciously fixed on my face. "Wait, what?" she asks.

I point at the game. "I was here with some friends last week, and this guy barreled in, screaming, bear hugged the Big Buck Hunter machine in the corner and tried to carry it out of here. I thought I remembered you from that night. I guess not."

Ridiculous, I know. But I must be on to something, because the icy suspicion in her face melts to a lukewarm curiosity. "What did he want it for?" she asks.

"Who knows? He was...crazy. I found out the next day he was an escaped mental patient from a nearby facility."

As she swirls her drink, which looks like a vodka lemonade, I notice Dusty smoothly slide up to her friend and say something, which induces an engaged giggle right out the gate. Now armed with the ideal wingman, I have no excuses.

I've got to keep this phony story going, keep her attention, then hopefully get her number.

"What happened, the police stopped him?" she asks.

"Didn't even have to. The game's gun was dangling on its cord. And *whack*. He trips over it. Falls down. Drags the machine with him. The whole thing slams onto the floor. That's why it's out of order."

"Oh my God." She giggles. As she laughs she closes her eyes and hides them, but I can see her smile. Then she sips her drink, and I can see her eyes but not her smile. I haven't made up my mind about which pose she looks more beautiful in. I don't think I'd ever be able to. It's a tie.

"Freaky, right? He got embarrassed I guess, then just ran out."

"Well, I definitely would've remembered that if I were here. You must have me mistaken for another girl." She looks around. "Which seems pretty hard to do at a place like this. There aren't many of us."

I chuckle and whisper, "And the ones who are here look like they pulled up on tractors."

She laughs.

"I'm guessing you're not from here," I say.

"Long Island. My family has a ski house a couple towns over. We're up for the weekend. I live in the city though. I go to NYU."

"I work in the city."

"Yeah, doing what?"

"Driving a limo."

"That always seemed hard to me. They're so big. How do you turn on those tight Manhattan streets without bumping into things?"

"It's a special gene. I was born with it. Under a microscope it looks like the Lincoln logo."

She kicks her head back and laughs louder than she has yet.

"I'm Brian," I say.

"Samantha."

"Well, Samantha, maybe I can pick you up from class at NYU one day in my limo, let all your friends think you're a really big deal. And as a token of appreciation, you can let me take you to lunch. What do you say?"

She holds her gaze on me. In her head I know complicated feminine machinery is analyzing my simple request from a plethora of angles, the sort of biological mechanisms fine-tuned by tens of thousands of years of evolution that intuitively and powerfully guide females toward romantic decisions.

Two seconds pass. Her eyelids slightly narrow. Five seconds. Her chin slightly tilts. Then, the results are in. "Sure," she says, "let me give you my number."

A euphoric rush surges through me as I slip my phone out of my pocket and take down Samantha's number. Once I save it I glance over at Dusty, my inspiration for taking this leap, hoping he saw what just went down.

Before I have the chance to discern any acknowledgement in his expression, a wall of purple and red blocks my view. I recognize the checkered colors, belonging to the flannel shirt of the zit-riddled dude who bumped into Dusty by the pool table earlier.

His body cleaves our foursome, Samantha and I on his right, Dusty and the brunette his left. "My friends and I couldn't help notice the two hotties at the bar," he says to the girls, his voice over-energetic. "We want to buy your next round. What're you drinking?"

"We're okay on drinks for now," Samantha says. "Thanks though."

"Come on. It's Friday night. You're supposed to be getting fucked up. It's on me. Shots? Tequila?"

"You heard her," the brunette tells him, her dainty voice hardening. "We're okay. Have a nice night."

"You don't have to be a bitch about it."

Her mouth hangs slightly agape at the escalation of his choice of words.

Dusty taps his shoulder. The guy turns around. "What the fuck did you just call her?" Dusty asks.

The guy, who's about thirty pounds heavier than Dusty and at six two about three inches taller, glares at him, his eyes wide-set and dilated, like a drunken shark's. "How old are you?" he asks Dusty.

"Twenty-four," Dusty tells him, his voice steady, not intimidated by the larger primate.

"Twenty-four ain't old enough to be her daddy. And if you ain't her daddy, you got no business minding what I call her."

"Well, how old are you?" Dusty asks.

"Twenty-eight."

"Twenty-eight is old enough to know how to avoid getting punched in the face."

"Huh?"

Dusty slams the toe of his boot into the guy's shin, the thud of rubber on bone audible to me even among the loud crowd. Grimacing, the guy bends forward. Dusty slugs him in the mouth, his knuckle striking the upper lip near the eye tooth, a line of blood spraying from his face.

The screech of chair legs. The screams of the girls. The sudden silence of the crowd. Dusty and him grapple, turning into one, a four-armed, four-legged animal, its shell the light blue of Dusty's shirt fused with the red and purple checkers of his opponent's.

I've never been in a fight in my life, but lunge toward them, hoping to help Dusty in some way, though totally unaware how. But as I do, two hands latch onto my shoulders. Turning, I see this guy's friend's earthworm scar, on a raging, red face.

I try to wiggle out of his grasp, but can't. He's too strong. Then I'm flying. My eyes close for a second, then shoot open. I'm on the floor. A ring in my ears. A pain in my forearm. I see human legs between the legs of the bar chairs, twenty, maybe more, scurrying, clearing away from me. My head throbs.

His waft of body odor jumps up my nose again. His two hands clench me again, hauling me across the floor, my shirt lifting up, the skin of my chest exposed, my rib bones clonking at the crevices between wooden planks.

I hear glass shatter. A fist comes at me. I roll left, just avoiding it. I launch my foot into the air and connect with the stomach of my attacker. The temperature cools a few degrees. I stand, my head wobbly and woozy.

Through my crooked vision, I spot Dusty. His chin is covered in blood. He throws a punch at the one in the purple-and-red shirt but misses. I see the shine of a fake diamond. I see something shinier near it. It's a bottle, broken, glinting as it glides through the air, the third member of the enemy trio brandishing it.

As I move out of the way, the bottle smashes on the edge of the bar, slivers exploding, a few falling down the collar of my shirt. He swings the jagged remains at Dusty's head. Dusty ducks, then uppercuts him in the gut.

I notice the New York Giants helmet on the bartender's sweatshirt hovering about. He's shouting. A dark-brown Louisville Slugger baseball bat is in his hands. All other voices hush, his dominating the space. "End it," I hear him say. "End it."

I'm breathing heavily yet can't hear myself breathe, my pulse so strong it's taken over the interior of my ears. I feel a hand on my shoulder. Dusty's. "Let's go," he says, his white teeth moving against the red backdrop of blood on his face. I follow him to the exit, the audience parting to make a path for us.

He cracks open the door, a gust of cold mountain air gushing inside, and turns to face the guys we fought. They stare at him. Everyone in the place stares at him.

His dirty-blond hair is frazzled, bent into points and twists. It looks like his head is on fire. His tee shirt is ripped at the collar, the upper portion of his torso bare. He's still, other than the slight swell and contraction of his exposed chest as he gets his breath back. For about eight seconds he's silent. Then leans forward and screams at the three guys, one continuous yell, no words, coarse and animalistic, out the cracked doorway and echoing throughout the mountains.

When his mouth is done screaming, it closes, then settles into a smile, his lips arched slightly at the right corner, a hint of white teeth among the red splatter on his face. He pushes the door fully open and steps into the night. I follow him.

So much adrenaline runs through my body that my brain's thoughts seem to dissolve in its wake. I don't think, just shake. Mindlessly, I tail Dusty as he trots along the side of the road, my feet landing in the footprints his make in the snow.

I don't ask where we're going. It's after midnight and the street is quiet, no cars, the windows on the nearby businesses dark. We walk for another minute or so. It must be near zero degrees. My breath puffs from my face as steam. However, though he's only in a tee shirt, a ripped one at that, I detect no signs of discomfort on Dusty from the cold. No shivering, no huddling, no wincing.

The big, rural silence breaks as the sound of a siren penetrates it. A blue-and-red crown of light rises from the horizon, spinning across the trees to our right and a snowy field with a chicken-wire fence to our left.

"C'mon," Dusty says, cutting right. He scales a snowy bank and disappears into the dark of the forest. I trail him. I can't make out his features but see his shape, a gray figure a few notches lighter than the knotty barks of the trees it's negotiating around, moving rapidly yet lightly. Like a phantom.

Two sirens are behind us now, their pitches and rhythms slightly off from one another, the combined noise frustrating my ears.

The terrain is slippery and inclined. I push branches out of my way, relying on just my right hand, my left still pulsating with pain from the fight. Dusty's phantom-like figure distances from me. The surface steepens.

Cold air fills my throat and hits my lungs like buckets of ice water. The phantom Dusty lunges over the top of a hill and I lose sight of him. I go faster. My legs burn with lactic acid, and though it hurts I like the warmth it ignites in my flesh. I go down on all fours and use my hands to propel myself the final few feet to the peak of the slope.

The ground flattens at the summit. I relax my wrists and let my body fall to the earth, the moisture in the snow bleeding through my shirt. I lie still for a half-minute catching my breath.

When I lift myself up I spot the phantom Dusty about forty feet in front of me, sitting on a log. I thump my chest, knocking the frost off, then walk through the forest toward him and take a seat on a log across. He shows no indication of fatigue. His hair still looks like it's on fire and his body seems warm. He peers at the moon above the snowy evergreens. A bird squawks in the distance.

"Let's hang up here for a while," he says. "Give the cops enough time to come and go from the bar. Then we'll go back down, grab my Jeep, and go home." He spits out some blood, dotting white snow red, then wipes his mouth with his fore-arm. "I at least got a couple good shots in." He grins. "You don't call a chick a bitch. You just don't do it."

Images of the bar fight flash in my mind. One picture keeps recurring, commanding the mental slideshow, the bro-ken beer bottle charging toward my head.

If I didn't move out of the way as quickly as I did, I could've been dead. If one of those glass edges caught me in the throat, I would've bled to death on the wooden-plank floor of Dakota Shirley's. Whether he was trying to kill me or not, he could've. He had no control over where exactly that bottle was landing. It hitting my jugular was just as likely as it ending up where it did.

I feel violated. How dare he? He could've killed me. *Killed* me. This stranger in a camouflage shirt with a fake earring, who doesn't know my name or where I'm from or what my family looks like, could've ended the life that the name, town, and family belong to. One swing of a bottle. An edge of glass meeting a piece of skin, a few seconds of bleeding, years lost, a wife never to meet her husband, children never to be born.

"Can you believe that piece of work with the broken bot-tle?" I ask.

"He was just a punk...don't mind him."

"I don't mind *him*. I mind the beer bottle he swung at both our heads like an ax. He missed you by six inches."

"Well...he still missed."

"If he hit you, you could've died."

A few moments pass. Then he says, "Dead or alive, it doesn't make sense to give a damn at this point. It's over."

We don't talk for a bit, then I chuckle and ask, "So you don't give a damn about dying?"

"I don't go around thinking about it, no."

"Well...that's just not human. And how can you not think about it after something like *that* happens?"

He lets out a long exhale and looks around the woods for a moment. "Thinking about dying is the worst way to live. You never even experience death. Nobody does. You experience the last few seconds of *living*, but you'll never endure your own death. You won't be here for it. You'll already be dead. Nothing to be scared of."

I hang my head, unable to formulate a response. By the time I lift it back up I notice Dusty is no longer on the log. Scanning the forest, I spot him striding toward the perimeter of the flat ground. He stops beneath a tall tree stripped of leaves. He leaps and grasps one of the branches with both hands.

"Dusty?" I shout, standing. He maneuvers along the limb toward the outside of the tree. "What the hell are you doing?" I scramble to him, seeing that the branch extends out over the edge of the terrain, a steep drop looming below. "Dusty, what the fuck?" He doesn't seem to even notice me. He shifts his right grip a few inches up the limb, then his left, then his right, then his left. He's now far enough out that if it snapped he'd go over. "Get down. Jesus Christ." My voice turns hoarse.

I debate physically stopping him, but don't want to tamper with him and put additional strain on the tree arm, which is now a shaking arch. "Come down, *now*," I yell. His eyes, which spark brighter than they have all night, stare at the rocky, watery grave beneath him. The peaceful sound of a stream carries up to us, agnostic of Dusty, indifferent to him living, indifferent to him dying.

The wind blusters, pushing his torn tee shirt to the side, exposing the bottom of his stomach. His chin is pressed to his chest, his hair in his face, his eyes fastened on the shadowy drop below him. He sways his legs backward, gaining some momentum, rocks twice, and lets go as he swings forward, the branch flying upward to its original position with a lashing noise. His left hip lands on the flat ground and he rolls in the snow.

On his back, he looks up at the moon. He wriggles, his hair and arms dragging in the dirt. I hear a sound coming from him. As I get closer I notice what it is.

Laughter.

Six

A loud voice snags my attention and I look toward it at the craps table. It shouts, "Come on, it's my birthday, I need a little luck on my birthday." The voice belongs to a tall, husky man in an off-white suit with a goatee and a homogenous layer of sweat spanning his forehead. I immediately recognize him, one of my passengers tonight, a new face I don't remember from the event last weekend.

Unlike the previous penthouse, which had a tony, old-money quality, this one in Tribeca has a trendy, youthful character. My passenger, who's sloshed, stands next to the croupier, speaking to him a little too closely, slurring every word. He cracks up at a bad joke he tells and looks around the table expecting the other players to join in on the laughter. None do, all seeming to find him obnoxious.

"Someone needs to tell that guy to ease up," Dusty says, over my shoulder. He wears a 1950s-style chauffeur hat, something he bought at a thrift shop that he'll occasionally throw on as part of the uniform.

"Yo," I say, seeing him for the first time since waking up on his couch this morning following last night's brawl in the mountains. We haven't talked of the fight or his subsequent stunt on the tree. He cooked us some eggs, which we ate while chatting about volcanoes, a topic he brought up, then I drove back to Jersey. And, oddly, it didn't feel like there was anything pending to discuss. Last night was behind us, undoubtedly imprinted on both of us, but behind us.

"I wonder when he got so drunk," I say. "He was dead sober in the limo before. It was no more than…" I check the time on my phone. "Thirty-five minutes ago."

Hard to look away, we watch the guy make a fool of himself for a while longer. It's entertainment. When the dice land he cracks another crappy joke to the croupier and gazes around the table awaiting laughs, and obtaining none. How doesn't he have a clue by now?

"Huh," Dusty says.

"What?"

"Look at Igor…watching him."

Scanning the crowd, I spot Igor eyeing the man from ten or so feet away. That toothpaste-commercial affability on his face last weekend is gone, replaced with the cold, blink-less focus of a bird of prey hiding in a treetop.

Dusty takes a step closer to the craps table and squints, his irises like little blue half-moons under his eyelids. "Holy shit."

"What?"

He spins around and slants his neck down, his mouth by my ear. "Check out the guy in the gray suit," he whispers.

Scoping the players circling the table, I notice one in gray. I recognize him too. He was with the drunk during my pickup before. Unlike his large, loud buddy, he's short and unassuming. The duo reminded me of Penn and Teller, the Vegas comedians, in my limo.

I study the smaller one for a bit, then tell Dusty, "He's just standing there, playing a couple numbers. I don't see anything weird about him."

"Wait until the big guy makes another joke."

I keep my eyes locked on the table for a couple minutes. The dice stop, and the big one's comedy routine continues. As the croupiers lean over to count the chips and pay the winners of the roll, he blurts, "Hey, what's six inches in length, two inches in width, and drives chicks crazy? Huh? A hundred-dollar bill." He erupts in laughter, patting the back of the croupier at his side.

And then I catch it, but just barely. The man in the gray suit, with a lightning-quick hand, slips an additional two chips on the table's "SIX" box. Sure enough, I check to see the number that came out on the roll and it was a six.

"They're working as a team," I say to Dusty, the tone of my voice slow and deliberate with my newfound understanding.

"The big one distracts the croupiers once the dice land. Before they pay out the winners, the shorter one slides an extra few chips on the number they know already won. These two guys wind up getting paid for winning a bet they never even made."

"He's probably not even really wasted."

Igor paces toward the table and taps the tall one on the shoulder. The phony drunk stupor he's been carrying on his expression immediately vanishes. Igor whispers something into his ear.

One of the gigantic guards appears at the craps table, seemingly out of nowhere, a difficult feat at nearly three hundred pounds of muscle, and calmly grabs the shorter fellow's forearm. Igor and his burly henchman, paying careful attention not to ruffle the crowd, begin escorting the scammers away.

Igor's hawkish eyes swivel around the room. They seem to stop on me. "You," he says.

My heart skips a beat.

I point at myself. He nods in confirmation, then says, "I need a driver. Let's go. Now."

A driver for what? Where does he plan to take these two? Whatever the answer, I don't want any part of its unfolding.

I'm sure Dusty would go for me if I asked. However, that would make me look weak. Guys like Igor, who apparently is in the mafia, don't like weak. Passing off this request could sink my reputation in his eyes and keep me out of future events and their four-figure compensation.

So I man up.

Buttoning my jacket, I wind through the attendees toward Igor. "Get your car," he tells me. "Pull up to the front of the building. We'll be down in two minutes. Hurry."

I give him a quick nod and stride to the elevator. I step in and select the lobby. On the ride down, I hope the lift is called on other floors. Those stops, even brief, would afford me a little extra time to sort my jumbled thoughts.

Luck is not on my side tonight. The elevator makes an uninterrupted descent to the ground floor, carrying nothing but me and my chaotic mind.

I cross the lobby and step into the cold. Walking to the garage where I parked, I pass quaint reminders of upcoming Christmas, buildings with velvety red wreaths on their faces, a Santa Claus collecting donations for a children's hospital, an Italian restaurant with a lit evergreen in its front window.

Once I retrieve the limo, I drive to tonight's event's apartment complex. Under the awning, in soft cones of entryway lighting, are Igor and the security guard with the two cheaters.

I coast to a stop and Igor opens the backdoor, letting his guests in first. Once they situate their stiff bodies in seats, the boss and his hulking sidekick get in, the door slamming behind them.

Igor provides me an address in an industrial part of Brooklyn, about a half hour away. Without a question, I embark toward it.

The interior of the long vehicle is quiet. I glimpse the rearview, receiving a partial view of the swindlers, their faces still and sullen.

"I don't know what you think you saw up there," the taller one says. "There were a lot of bets on the table. Things get confusing. My friend put a couple chips down a little too early. Honest mistake."

"Who made an honest mistake?" Igor asks.

"My friend did, sir. Right, Bobby?"

"That's all it was," the shorter conman says. "A mistake. My mistake."

"I must've made a mistake too, then," Igor says. "That's the implication of what you're telling me. My mistake, it seems, was misjudging your mistake. See, what I saw you do did not look to me like an error. It looked to me like something entirely different. But you're telling me this was an error in judgment on my part. Do I have this correct? Are you saying I made a mistake?"

The limousine is hushed for about ten seconds.

"Let's make this easy," the taller says. "Whatever you think you saw, however much money you think came our way that we didn't deserve, just let me know and I'll write you a check. Heck, and add ten percent on top of it. We can call it an inconvenience fee. My place isn't far from here. I'll run up, get my checkbook, and we can end this now. Driver. Hey, driver..."

I glance at him in the rearview.

"You mind making a quick detour?" he asks.

"Continue as you were, Brian," Igor says.

And I do.

"You still haven't answered my question," Igor says to the scammers. "It's an important question. Which seems to be at the heart of this predicament you've gotten yourselves into. And it's as equally simple as it is important. I'll pose it again. Are you saying I made a mistake?"

Quiet for a while.

"Well," the taller answers in a hesitant tone. "It was a misunderstanding, and if you want to call a misunderstanding a mistake, then yes, I guess, technically, I am saying that. I'm saying you made a mistake."

More quiet.

"I appreciate your candor," Igor says. "I'm a trusting man, and I'd like to give you a chance to prove your assertion to me. I don't know if you're aware, but before my events start, my staff plants cameras around the venue. I have one on each table, recording all night. If what you're saying is correct, that your friend made one innocent, early bet, the camera would of course show that. And we can say I made a mistake. However, the camera could also show something else. It could show him placing a series of early bets. And it could also show you trying to distract my croupier at the exact times he did this. In that case, we can deem that neither of us made a mistake. It'd be clear that what you two were up to wasn't an honest error, but a calculated ploy. And it'd be clear that I made no error in uncovering it. The footage is all digital. I can call my staff and have it emailed to my phone in a couple minutes. We can watch it together. Right here in the limousine. Should I make that phone call?"

Again, the car is silent for a while.

"Whatever happened, happened," the taller says, his voice now a touch trembly. "The past is the past whether it's on some videotape or not. I want to look ahead. To the future. To making this all right. I mentioned a ten-percent inconvenience fee before. Let's make this easy. Up it to twenty. Why am I doing all the talking, anyway? You're the one the money is going to. You tell me. You tell me how much you want. Let's figure this out. What's it going to take to forget about this?"

"Who invited you tonight?"

"What do you mean?"

"To my event. I've never seen you or your associate before. I do allow guests I trust to extend a minimal amount of invitations to their trusted friends. And I'm wondering, what guest told you about tonight?"

"Just...you know...you know how these things go...the grapevine, heard it through the grapevine you can say."

"I take very specific precautions to assure people do not hear about my functions through the...*grapevine*. And I believe those precautions, widely, are effective. My events are attended by a network of respectable, like-minded, trusted individuals, who do not like when that sense of trust is broken. And nothing erodes their sense of trust more than outsiders sneaking in. For instance, two-bit sleazes who tricked their way into learning about the night's pickup locations and password. It'd be terrible if you happened to be people like that. I'm already a bit offended you tried to steal from me. Finding out you sneaked into my function on the same night would only offend me further. I don't like being offended. I've been known to act rather unpredictably when I'm offended."

"We meant no offense to you, sir. We know who you are. The last thing we wanted to do was offend someone like you. Truly. We're sorry. We're sorry for this entire hassle."

Igor says nothing back. Nobody does for the next twenty or so minutes as I drive into Brooklyn.

We pass a bunch of pubs, crowds of cigarette-smoking hipsters congregated on the sidewalks out front. Over the following few blocks, the count of bars dwindles, soon turning to nothing.

Buildings surround us, but none open, a mixture of the boarded-up, graffiti-scarred, and abandoned, and faded-brick factories still in operation but closed at these hours. No people working in any windows or walking on any roads.

"Pull in here," Igor says as I approach an alley. I turn in, the limo enclosed by a barbed-wire fence on the left and a moonlight-striped warehouse wall on the right. The scent of day-old trash, powerful enough to transcend window glass, hits us from a nearby dumpster.

"This is good," Igor tells me. "Park."

I do.

"And leave the engine running," he adds.

I do.

In the rearview, I notice him climb across the leather seats to the limo's mini bar. He grabs four glasses and a bottle of Macallan whisky.

"I've been thinking on the ride," he tells his two guests. "And you're right. We should put this behind us. Let's get some air and have a drink now that we came all the way out here. When we go back to the event, we can come to a financial arrangement to clear this all up. An inconvenience fee as you called it. Clever name, by the way. That's the most sensible path."

"I am so glad you see things the same way as us, sir," the tall one says, a streak of rejoicing in his voice.

Igor opens the door, letting the two guests out first, then his security guard, then exits himself. I turn around, watching the four of them through the limo's long side window. Igor passes the others glasses, opens the bottle, and fills each with two fingers of liquor. He raises his cup and they all clink, smiles on all their faces.

Then the smile on the tall cheater goes limp as Igor hammers the whisky bottle into his forehead. His big frame plummets to the pavement, where it's immediately met in the sternum by the toe of Igor's dress shoe.

A nervous scream emits from the other's mouth, which stops as the security guard's cannonball fist bashes his teeth. The henchman mounts the fallen body and proceeds to jerk it up and down, the rear of the skull cracking into the asphalt each repetition.

My conscience tells me to hit the gas of the still-running limousine and get out of here. As the driver, I'm now associated with this violent ambush. Racing away would absolve me of any guilt.

However, ditching Igor out here next to two bloody bodies could be disastrous. First, he'd surely terminate my stint as a casino driver. Then, who's to say he wouldn't turn my body into a third bloody one once he eventually caught up to me?

So I stay put. But my entire being hates me for it. Nausea whirls in my stomach, working its way up my esophagus. I free the driver's door and vomit out the chicken dinner my mother made me before I came into the city.

The door open, I can hear the sound of the beating even clearer, the thud of flesh as it absorbs the leather of a shoe, the thwack of bone as it bangs into pavement.

I lean back inside. Soon, Igor and the security guard join me in the limo, leaving their victims behind. They're alive, but not by much, life indicated by only the slight respiratory rise of their chests.

"Okay, Brian," Igor says, his voice composed. "Back to Tribeca."

"Yes, sir," I say, putting the car in drive.

Seeing my reflection in the rearview, I gawk at how terrible I look. Pale and pulled. My accomplice guilt consumes me, on the inside and out.

I got into this gambling thing to save my brother from gang violence. In doing so, I've turned into an enabler of it.

Morally, it was difficult for me to first drive the events, to flirt with illegality of any kind. But now I've gone way further, prostituting myself to the cause. Though gambling isn't allowed in New York, it's a victimless crime. But what I just helped enable has two very definite, very wounded victims.

Sure, my brother's physical safety is more important than my mental health. But the consequences of this side job are now much more treacherous than anxiety. After what I just helped facilitate, if I continue down this road, more than my mind will be in jeopardy.

My whole soul will.

Seven

The Sunday-morning air of Pramin Township is brisk, versus flat-out cold, the few-degree difference making a cup of coffee out on a porch rocking chair surprisingly enjoyable in mid-December.

The half-dozen acres of property Dusty's modest rental cabin sit on stretch wide before us under a sheet of thinning snow, its uniform whiteness interrupted only by the occasional gold ray of the newly risen sun atop the Catskill Mountains.

"He's a professional criminal," Dusty, in a rocking chair next to mine, both of them his handmade creations, says. "But simple association with Igor doesn't make you one too. That's not who you are. It *is* who he is."

Last night, after I returned to the Tribeca penthouse from the alley in Brooklyn, I was of course quite shook up. I told Dusty what I witnessed and how I felt and he told me he's there to talk, that I should drive up to Pramin after the event and crash at his place. Desperate for someone's ear, mum to my mom's, dad's, and brother's about this stuff, I agreed.

Since I've been driving at Big Hitter, I liked Dusty. But he was only an acquaintance, a co-worker. However, the last couple weeks, since I reached out to him for help about my brother, acquaintance no longer feels apt. This has evolved into a friendship. Unquestionably the most interesting of my life.

"My dad's a cop," I say. "I told you that. He used to tell us stories all the time growing up, about how good people can make a few bad choices and get sucked into the worlds of bad people. And never get out. Being around someone like Igor, working for him, having to obey his orders, puts me in a place where I'm susceptible to bad choices. No, I'll never turn into a professional criminal. But that doesn't mean I still can't change into something else...something I don't like."

"If you quit, what happens to your brother?"

I lift the coffee mug to my mouth, letting the hot drink soak into my taste buds for a few seconds before swallowing. I don't answer Dusty's question because I don't know how to. If I quit, I really have no idea what the next steps would be for Kip.

Dusty, who can clearly tell he struck a nerve, shifts subjects, saying, "You wanted to see the workshop, right? C'mon, I'll show you."

I follow him to the cabin's garage, which he converted into a furniture-building haven. I assumed he'd have a hammer and a couple pieces of lumber in here, however it's much more than that.

Wood slabs in dozens of lengths rest against the far wall, two DeWalt mechanical saws side by side on the near wall, and against the third, a shelf packed with tools and supplies, three drills, a bottle of glue, two metal wedges, four chisels, a handheld belt sander, a tin can with seven screwdrivers and paintbrushes poking out, three hammers, two sheets of sand-paper, five cans of Minwax wood stain, and a plastic jug of West Marine paint thinner.

He flips on a circular space heater, about a foot in diameter, which sits on the floor among a bed of wood shavings.

Secured in vices on his workbench is the top of an in-progress table. As he approaches it, he says, "This is basically where I've been spending all my time when I haven't been working...or getting into bar fights with you."

I chuckle. "It's really cool. I know nothing about this sort of stuff."

"This here," he says, picking up a metal tool, "plays a big part. Called a hand plane." He begins running the hand plane over the tabletop.

"What's the point of doing that?"

He scrutinizes the texture of the wood. His light eyes, combined with his dark eyebrows, when in this pensive state, give him the aura of a jungle cat. He blows on the surface, a cloud of dust rising and settling, then gets back to action with the hand plane, focusing on an area at the top-right corner of the tabletop.

"It's very important," he tells me. "Very. It smoothes the wood. Gives it that *exact* right look."

He says "exact" with a sense of both clarity and craving in his voice, as if he has a precise vision of what he wants, and wants nothing more than achieving it. Yet, I can't tell what he's searching for when he studies the wood. What did he notice on the top-right corner that needed adjustment? He simply sees something I don't. He's a woodworker and I'm not.

It's still so bizarre to me that he's so into all this. "How did you get involved with making furniture?" I ask.

He doesn't reply, pushing and pulling the hand plane, and I don't believe he heard me. Then after a few seconds he answers, "About ten years ago. When the desk in my bedroom broke. We didn't have enough money for a new one. So I figured I'd try making one."

"And you were just able to...make a desk...out of nowhere?"

"I was working with wood for about two years before that." He kneels for another texture inspection.

Eager to get to the root of this hobby, I keep probing, "Did you have a part-time job or something, with a carpenter, when you were a kid?"

"Not quite." He slides his fingertips over a three-inch spot in the middle of the slab. "I built a tree house."

"You learned how to do all *this* building a tree house when you were twelve?" I made a tree house when I was twelve too, and don't know how to hand carve fluted legs in a dining set now.

"This was no ordinary tree house. It wasn't even really mine. It was my friend Dan's. We used his backyard. His dad worked in construction. He bought us all the supplies, and taught us the basics. That summer, Dan and I put up a decent tree house. Block steps. One small room. Window. Roof." He brushes some hair out of his face. "What we built was cool. But...then, it was one of those things..." His voice fades and he laughs in a way I've never heard him laugh, softly and defensively. "I kept going back to Dan's after we were done. To add things. He helped me at first, but by the time school started in the fall, he was done with it. But the family let me keep coming to the backyard. I made a second room. Peaked roof. Back staircase. Mr. Logan...Dan's dad...didn't mind buying me more supplies. He knew how much I liked it, not to mention I was building this great thing in his yard that his son would hang out in. Winters in Missouri got rough. So I took some time off, but was back that spring. Dan helped me, but at that point I'd gotten so much better than him he became an assistant, not a partner. So yeah. I wound up getting pretty decent at it, you could say."

"You kept going back because you knew it was making you better at woodworking, or you just really liked the tree house?"

"Both to a degree. But neither at first." He gazes at the unfinished tabletop. "It started as an excuse not to be at home." With his eyes on mine he nods twice, gently, almost unnoticeably, then sets his hand plane back on the wood and pushes it, the scrape of the tool and whirr of the space heater the only noises in the garage.

"Why didn't you want to be home?"

The hand plane moves faster than it's been, the muscles in his forearm tensing, shapes of veins showing under the skin. He finally stops thrusting it, standing motionless with his knuckles on his hips.

"My mom was a good woman," he says. "*Was.* But my dad ruined her. Hit her. A lot. It must've eaten at her over the years. She lost whatever...verve she had when I was really young. In most of these cases people blame alcohol, right? Oh, so and so, he's just a nasty drunk. My dad didn't even drink. He was no nasty drunk. Just a nasty guy."

This explains why Dusty freaked out at Dakota Shirley's Friday night when that local called Samantha's friend a bitch. Dusty grew up in close quarters with a woman abuser.

"That's terrible," I say. "I had no clue you had to put up with that."

"Well, I decided to stop putting up with it at seventeen. Before I even finished high school I took a bus to New Orleans, got a job as a bar-back, and haven't spoken to my parents since."

"You were okay all on your own, that young?"

"Was refreshing to get out of small-town Missouri. I liked New Orleans a lot. Then it was on to Nashville. Baltimore. Now New York. I haven't looked back and don't plan to stop. That's why I'm driving the gambling events. Why I put up with Igor and the rest of it. I'm saving money to travel. First America, then the world. I want to do it while I'm still young. See the work of all the great sculptors up close. Rome, Paris, Barcelona. It'll take my woodworking to places I can only imagine. Not to mention, all the other experiences. All those cities around the world. Each just waiting there. Waiting for you to come and grab your little piece of it."

As I watch Dusty stand there with the hand plane in his grip, tabletop project at his side, and goal of global travel in his head, my entire life flashes before my eyes and I realize how screwed up I've pictured it all.

I've been operating under the assumption that if you did what the conventions of society wanted you to do, one day in the future things would just fall into place and the world would grant you happiness.

Dusty's entire existence stands in contradiction to that. Society never gave him anything as a child and he has no reason to think it will as an adult. He's on a mission to make his own happiness. And he's not relying on some vague hope that life will eventually fall into place, but focusing on specifics. Woodworking and world travel. The man knows what he wants and doesn't give a damn if he has to break society's conventions by driving for an illegal casino in order to get it.

Igor can't change Dusty's soul because Dusty's soul is too well defined. Mine, I unfortunately realize, still needs a lot of work. Since high school I've just been going through the motions, waiting for life to give me something versus taking something from life. Of course I always wanted to make money. But what exactly would I spend it on if I had it, other than basics like my own apartment? What's my passion, my woodworking?

I sadly don't know. I've been in too thick a fog the last decade to have even seen the question. But I see it now. Thanks to Dusty, I see it now.

And in this moment I decide I'm going to keep driving the gambling events. Until I earn enough to liberate my brother from his debt. I can't be afraid of Igor changing my soul. From now on, the only person who has anything to say about Brian Rolson's soul is me.

Eight

As I walk along Spring Street toward the SoHo building where tonight's gambling event is, I can't stop thinking about Samantha.

She's been on my mind since I dropped her off at her dorm yesterday after our lunch date. Mainly the kiss she left me with. Quick and tasteful, yet definitely on the lips versus the cheek, in the romance zone versus the friend one, the place that's confined all previous relationships I've had with girls who look close to how good Samantha does.

I enter the complex, check in, and ascend to the penthouse. The couches are made of leather and chrome and the chairs are shaped into clear-plastic letters, "G," "X," and "J" noticeable from this angle. Film-set-style spotlights shine on the gambling tables, yet no other lights are on, so the alleys between the action are dim, as are the walls, which are covered in black-and-white photographs of consumer-staple cans and cartons from grocery stores.

Peppy voices of craps players encircle me as I wander deeper into the main room. "Eight the hard way, three thousand." "Odds on the five, press the six." "Boxcars."

Unbuttoning my jacket, I make out Dusty in the corner, sitting on one of the letter-shaped seats, the "H," about a dozen feet to the rear of a roulette wheel, watching it spin under its spotlight as he sips a soda. He's far enough away from the table where the light beam doesn't reach him, and seems like he's floating, the see-through chair material nearly invisible in the shadows.

I wind through the crowd, my coat tucked between my hip and arm, and sit next to him, on the "S."

"Yo," I say.

He waves without making eye contact, his attention bolted to the roulette table. He lifts the glass of Coke to his lips and drinks, then passes it to me. It's likely spiked, yet I don't care about drinking on the job like I did the night of the first event when he offered me that flask. I have a swig, the sharp taste confirming the presence of vodka.

Handing the cocktail back to him, I watch the white ball whip around the mahogany rim of the roulette wheel and the six expectant faces of the huddled players anticipating its fate. It spins so fast you can't even tell it's a ball, then slows slightly, loops a couple more times, almost finishes another revolution, and drops, banging into a diamond-shaped silver bumper, striking another, smacking against the red "21" slot, popping out, and settling on black "31." The facial features of half the players deflate into relief, while the expressions of the others are stiff watching the white ball rotate among the borders of black "31."

"It's a scam if you ask me," I tell Dusty.

"What now?"

"All this. Gambling."

"How so?"

"The house always wins," I say, elongating my pronunciation of "always."

He has a sip of the drink and says, "With a scam someone gets the wool pulled over their eyes. They have no idea what they're getting into. These people know *exactly* what they're getting into." He nods at the roulette players. "I guarantee you every one of them is a master of the roulette rule book. The board, the bets, the odds. Everything. And they choose to play at their own will. How is that a scam?"

"They may know the odds but that doesn't change that the odds are tilted against them. We learned about this sort of business model in college. It's called statistical arbitrage."

"Statistical arbitrage...sounds like a part in one of Doc Brown's time machines." He situates the heel of his right shoe on his left knee, while his hands hang off the clear armrests of the "H" seat, the drink dangling from his grip.

With a chuckle I say, "Look it up. The odds are in favor of the house on *every* bet. Roulette, craps, blackjack. Sure, gamblers can go on lucky streaks. But the more they play, the larger the sample size is, the more likely they are to lose in aggregate. It's been proven and proven. Gambling is irrational. I can't understand why any of these people would do it."

"You're saying they're stupid?"

"No...I just...there's just no logic behind it, is what I'm getting at."

He looks me in the eye. "They're here, they gamble, because they like the feeling they get in the moment. The feeling when the ball is about to land. That's it. Statistics have nothing to do with it. When you play, you don't have to think. And to most people, thinking...*really* thinking...is the most stressful thing in the universe."

I muse on this for a bit, not entirely sure what he means.

He points at the table, the ball circling again, and says, "When you're playing the world is small, divided into red and black and the thirty or so numbers on the wheel. The ball spins, and all that matters is where it lands. An outcome you have no control over. The players act like they have strategies for choosing numbers, but deep down they know it's random. They know it has nothing to do with them. And that's why they're there. They don't need to make any decisions in that world. The only panic in that world is the brief moment before the ball falls. It's safe panicking. A safe rush. An easy rush. And if you ask me...a sad one."

A waitress visits the roulette group, asking them if they need refills, the beam from the spotlight ricocheting our way off the empty glasses on her tray.

She halts as Igor's voice overtakes the space, screaming, "Listen up. We need to evacuate. *Now.*"

Looking over my shoulder, I notice him at the front of the room signaling everyone toward the hallway. "Let's go," he hollers.

Pandemonium. Gamblers grope for their stacks of chips, stuffing them in pockets and purses. Toward the exit a stampede ensues, barreling over the metal spotlights.

"C'mon," Dusty yells, the "H" chair toppled on its side next to him. I tail him through the dense drove, a cord of anxiety squeezing the meat of my heart.

A knee hits my thigh. An elbow digs into my spine. Cologne. Perfume. Body odor.

A woman to my left in high heels slips on a spilt martini, her left leg lost beneath her. She shrieks as she stumbles toward the floor. I grab her under the armpits just in time to keep her up.

"I got you," I say. "Here." I offer my hand and usher her toward the foyer.

"Stairs," Igor screams. "Everyone must leave down the *stairs*."

I try to peek around the wide shoulders of the man in front of me to see what's going on but the visibility is weak, affording not much more than napes of necks and shapes of hairdos.

"Bri," I hear Dusty call. I make out a portion of his dirty-blond head ahead in the flock.

"Behind you," I call back.

"Richard," the woman I'm with cries out to a man I assume is her husband. She lets go of me and shuffles, against the current of the crowd, to him.

Everyone attempts to squeeze through a two-and-a-half-foot-wide space into the stairwell. Dozens of bodies are between the door and me, packed tight and at strange angles, like pieces of timber in a logjam. I come to a standstill, unable to push my way any farther through the thick throng.

I hear shouting to my right. About ten people wave claim tickets at Zlata, the elderly lady who runs the cashier area. "Number fourteen," a man says, bits of saliva spraying from his mouth. "I'm not leaving without my briefcase. I have eleven grand cash in there." Little Zlata bustles to collect the claim tickets and fetch the numbered cases.

Nearby, Igor directs two guards in Russian as they unlock the safe. One of the men runs into the kitchen, soon returning with two big Hefty bags. The guards load the money from the safe into the bags as Igor stomps his foot and smacks his hands, urging them to go faster.

My eyes shift from the cash to the exit door. I'm only fifteen feet away. I can feel the winded man behind me huffing, his breath heavy against my neck. I'm so narrowly sandwiched that I'm no longer walking, but advancing in a waddle. We all inch toward the stairwell. Twelve feet. Nine. Seven.

"Everyone freeze," a voice commands. The tone is different than Igor's, the accent not Russian but American, pure New York. "Stomachs on the floor. Hands behind your backs. All of you. Now."

I see an assault rifle. Then another. And another. The cord around my heart tightens. Rushing out of the elevator are NYPD officers in bulletproof vests with "POLICE" across the chest, black helmets with face shields, bulky forearm protectors from elbow to wrist, shin versions from knee to ankle.

As the five policemen storm into the penthouse, we all stop in our tracks. The hinges of the stairwell door squeak, then the slab slams shut.

"Get the fuck down," one of the cops barks as he gestures toward the floor with his gun. I place my quivering hands on the hardwood, discarded drinks seeping through my shirt and chilling my chest, then interlock them behind my back, the twenty or so remaining guests doing the same.

I see the pale faces of gamblers stuck to the floor and the black shoes of NYPD officers stamping around, my nose close enough to pick up the rubbery scent of some soles.

All the non-police in the apartment are now facedown, except one person.

Igor.

With a smirk, he stands tall under the archway separating the hallway from the main room. I crane my neck for a better view. Three gun-drawn officers charge his way, one patting him down while the others part off toward the gaming tables.

The two sweep the main room. *Woomack.* A banging noise. *Dabunk.* Another. Through the archway I see a roulette wheel crash onto the floor, its numbers spinning as it wobbles. One of the cops kicks a blackjack table over, its cards flying toward the ceiling, spades and diamonds and kings and queens twirling through the air. Under the officers' clear face shields I make out smiles. They're enjoying this.

The elevator doors open, the patter of a new pair of footsteps entering the apartment. It's another cop, not equipped in combat gear like the rest but slacks and loafers, an NYPD windbreaker on top of a starched white shirt and neatly knotted navy-blue tie. He pauses a couple feet to my side, positioning his hands on his hips, exposing the detective badge fixed to his belt.

"Good evening Mr. Krevanov," he says to Igor. The cop peeks into the main room, chuckling at the overturned tables and the cluttered cards around them. "Sorry if we scratched anything."

"Don't worry about it," Igor says. "I can buy new ones. It was time for an upgrade anyway."

The detective paces along the hardwood between the belly-down bodies. "I'm sure you could afford new ones. You've been bringing in a lot of money with this little operation I assume."

"We sure have."

The cop keeps his gaze on Igor for a few seconds, then snaps his fingers at one of the guests on the floor and says, "You. Get up." As he rises I see who it is, the white-haired man who asked Dusty about his furniture building the night of my first event. "Grab it," the detective insists, pointing at the briefcase by his feet. "And open it."

The guy dials a three-digit combination on a gold panel to the left of the handle, and another on a gold panel to the right. He peels the top back revealing a cluster of hundreds, about ten grand worth. The cop rips the case from him and tips it over, the money spilling out, the bills landing on the backs of the people beneath, some on Dusty's.

"I've got you inside a private residence with tables, players, and…cash," the detective says to Igor, with a cocky leer. "This casino has officially taken its last bet."

"You wouldn't be much of a humanitarian if you let that happen, officer."

The detective laughs. He wipes his nose. "Arrest him," he tells one of the officers. Drawing his handcuffs, the cop approaches Igor.

"Do you consider yourself a humanitarian?" Igor asks the detective.

The policeman stops before cuffing him. He glances at his boss. The boss nods and asks Igor, "What the fuck are you talking about?"

"I'm guessing you haven't heard of a lovely organization called America's Hearts for Russia's Hurt." Igor gestures toward the white-haired guest. "Yes, Vincent here was playing cards tonight. As were many other good-natured New Yorkers. They were doing it for charity. I host casino nights, where generous American businesspeople buy chips for cash and become eligible for donated prizes. The cash collected is driven to the headquarters of the charity on the Upper East Side before the gambling even begins. The charity then allots the funds to homeless shelters throughout Russia. It's a wonderful cause. If the NYPD is interested in donating a prize for the next event, let me know and I'll put you in touch with my secretary."

The detective slides his thumb and index finger down the sides of his chin, then points at the safe, butted against the wall at an uneven angle. "Unlock it," he tells Igor.

Igor slowly strides across the hallway, facedown gamblers nudging to make a path for him. He wheels the safe front and center, goes down to a knee, and keys in the access code. Standing, he points at the door and tells the detective, "Please, have a look."

The cop and criminal hold their gazes on each other for a few seconds, then the officer swings open the door, seeing the safe is empty.

"As I mentioned," Igor says through a smirk, "the players bring cash, but the house doesn't keep a cut for itself. And the last time I checked New York's casino laws, that's what determines if a gambling event is illegal or not."

The detective's tongue rolls around in his mouth, its outline squirming underneath the skin of his cheeks. "I need all the paperwork and the financial history for this...US Hearts for Russian—"

"America's Heart for Russia's Hurt."

"Whatever. Get me the documents. Immediately."

Igor disappears inside a guest bedroom and returns with a thick accordion folder, on it a sticker for the charity with a logo and everything.

He hands it over. The detective snickers and says, "I'm going to have the best accountants at City Hall go through these bogus records line for line. You've made a mistake somewhere in here, Krevanov. We'll find it. And when we do you'll see me again." He peers at his five men scattered throughout the apartment, then nods toward the elevator.

As the policemen congregate, Igor says, "Between then and now, if the NYPD is interested in donating anything at all for a future event, please don't hesitate to get in touch. I'm assuming you have all my contact information at this point."

The elevator car opens and the cops pack inside. The detective looks out at the rest of us on the floor. His eyes stop on me. Just before the elevator doors close he winks at me, tauntingly, like how a batter would wink at a rival pitcher before stepping up to the plate.

About twenty of us are out here. Why me?

A glint of recognition in his expression gives me the feeling he's seen me before, though I'm certain I've never seen him. That wink wasn't random.

It was for me and nobody else. And I have no idea why.

Nine

The slow, peaceful tune diffusing from the piano of Le Petit Pont, an upscale French bistro a short walk from the penthouse, doesn't stop the wild propulsion of my nerves, but does steady them a touch, sort of like one of those parachutes that pops from the rear of a hundred-fifty-mile-an-hour drag-racing car.

After the cops left, tonight's event effectively ended. Freaked out, the guests got the hell out of there, some muttering comments about never returning to Igor's casino again. Needing a place to think, needing a place to drink, Dusty and I stumbled into here, the first establishment we saw that looked like it served alcohol. Also in need of some mental decompression, Dusty's pal Vince Berrini, the guest who had his suitcase poured out by the cops, came along.

The three of us sit around a circular table, impatiently waiting for the waiter to deliver the much-needed first round we just ordered. A candle burns in a red-glass orb toward the center of the surface, a wave of light oscillating across Vince's full head of white hair.

After the first shot, Vince, who clearly has a lot more on his mind than the casino raid, starts talking about his ex-wife. With anger in his voice, he says, "All my life, 'Baby, whatever you want, it's yours.' And I worked for it. I built that business up from nothing. It was for her. All for her. And *this* is what she does to me. Mink coat? You got it. New Mercedes convertible? You got it. Membership at a Waspy tennis club? I'm not a Wasp and I don't play tennis. But it doesn't matter. You got it. Vacation house in Florida so you can be close to your mother who, God forbid, could ever get on an airplane and fly two hours to New York to see you up here? You got it. Whatever she wanted. Thirty-seven years. And I catch her in bed with this...fuck...this...not much older than you two. Younger than all three of my kids. This...I can't...and she has the nerve to tell me that I wasn't *around* enough. That she wasn't feeling *wanted*. That I was *too* much into my business. Which provided her everything she asked for. What is that? Huh? You tell me. What is *that*?"

After the second shot, he continues talking about her but the current of anger in his voice is replaced by one of guilt. He says, "You do things, and you get into a...motion...and...maybe I could've played less poker. Maybe, I don't know, maybe a night here and a night there. Was she justified to do *this*? Absolutely not. But am I saying I was the *perfect* husband? Who is, you know? Who's *always* there? Now the kids. It breaks my heart. One in California, one in Florida with her mother and her grandmother, then one in Jersey, Ridgewood, twenty minutes from me in my big empty townhouse in the City. I call him up, 'Anthony, come and visit. Bring Donna. Bring the baby. I'll order in dinner. Whatever you want.' I *beg*. I'm lucky if I see him on the holidays. My grandson too. My wife...my *ex*-wife...

turned them all on me. I'm the bad guy now. Because I wasn't the perfect husband. Could I have been better? Sure. Did I deserve this? After building a life for all of them? No. But could I have been better? Sure. Sure."

We do another shot. And another. I'm drunk. Which I guess is good. I needed it right now. First, to get my head off the mayhem of the raid. Second, to get my head off the mystery behind that fucking cop's wink.

Vince is nice enough to pick up the sizable tab which, based on his ownership of the American Express Black Card he pays with, isn't all that sizable to him. And a few minutes later Dusty and I are in his limo, giving Vince a lift back to his townhouse to thank him.

Dusty drives, with me riding shotgun and Vince alone in the big, glitzy back. Hearing a rustling noise behind me, I turn around, noticing Vince pulling a small baggie of cocaine from his coat. He empties some on his briefcase and sucks it into his nose with a hundred-dollar bill.

He wipes his right nostril and stares out the window at the West Village. "I used to date a girl who lived in that building," he says, pointing at a non-descript brown high-rise. "This is before I started my business. I was still working at a drugstore in Jersey City. I was...seventeen, still in high school. I'd take the bus into New York to see her. Only lasted one summer. She was nineteen. I lied. Told her I was twenty-one. Maria Morado was her name."

Silence. "Is that right?" I ask, letting him know someone's at least listening to him.

"She was a great one. She'd cook for me every time I came over. She didn't really know what she was doing, she was just learning, but I liked it. I liked the whole thing of it. I'd sit on the couch, and have some wine, and she'd be in the kitchen with these recipes her Sicilian grandmother wrote down for her, trying to make them right. I remember the pieces of paper they were on. Not quite the notebook kind. It was thin, like something you'd sketch on, but still had little lines, almost invisible, so you could write letters if you wanted. And the grandmother scribbled out the recipes in Italian. The paper was so fine it would have these blue inkblots all over. Would bleed right through. But Maria didn't mind. She'd squint to make sure she saw every ingredient. Every amount. She tried so hard to get it right. Sometimes she'd tell me to come over at seven, and we wouldn't wind up eating till nine thirty. I'd have a bottle and a half of wine in me after waiting on the couch. I remember looking out the window. It was that window right there." He points back at the building, but we're too far up the road to see where exactly he's pointing. "I'd look outside while I was on the couch, with the smell of sauce next to me in the kitchen, and I was only seventeen at the time, younger than you both, and I remember thinking how...big...things were, how big life is, how much more of it I had. You know? You ever do that? Just think how *big* it is?" He doesn't speak for a few seconds, then continues, "I haven't seen her since that summer. Over the years, on nights when I was alone, up and couldn't sleep, or taking a long drive home by myself, I'd imagine Maria. Not because I wanted to find her or anything.

Or leave my wife for her. It was…sometimes I just liked think-ing of her. Of her apartment. And that couch. And the window. Just to have the thought of it. I still do that sometimes."

He goes quiet staring at the buildings as they pass, many of which look exactly like the one Maria Morado used to live in.

In a bit we drop him off in front of his place, a three-story townhouse about three times the size of my parents' home in Dingan. The windows are all dark. He gets out and waves. We wave back, thanking him again for the drinks, and watch him go inside.

Dusty swings me over to the garage where I parked and I drive my limo back to Big Hitter in Queens, exchanging it for my Hyundai Sonata.

I'm a bit buzzed on the trip back to Jersey, but make it just fine on the empty, middle-of-the-night roads. I park in the driveway and gently open the side door, being careful to keep my noise level well beneath anything that may stir my sure-to-be-asleep mom, dad, and brother.

I enter the tiny coat-closet hallway off the kitchen, in my periphery the view of our Christmas tree in the den, the tran-quil glow from its wrapped light strands illuminating the hung family portrait we posed for nine years ago, my parents' adult faces with a few less wrinkles, and the faces of Kip and me, aged ten and thirteen, with nothing adult in them at all, con-sumed entirely by boyish smiles.

This was before Kip changed. When he was still a happy kid. Before he was teased in middle school for being skinny and unathletic, before the defensive shell sprouted out of him in high school that desperately wanted to be viewed as tough and serious, and eventually pushed him down the path of dealing cocaine.

As I approach the staircase to my bedroom, as my view of the den widens, a second image of my father crashes into sight, not another inanimate one like the one in the painting, but the one-and-only living, breathing kind.

He sits on an armchair and I at first assume he's sleeping, that he drifted off down here watching a movie. However, under the heavy shadow across his face, I see the whites of two well-awake eyes.

The television is off. No books, magazines, or papers are at his side, no plates of midnight snacks. He just sits there, at past four o'clock in the morning.

"Hey dad," I say.

He remains statue-like, no movement to his limbs or mouth.

"What the heck are you doing?" I ask.

Nothing back from him.

"You all right, dad?"

About ten seconds go by. Then he says, "A charity?"

"Huh?"

"You have the nerve to use that as an excuse? A charity?"

"What charity?"

"These people you're working for. They rob, they intimidate, they murder. If they just came out and said that, I'd loathe them, but at least you could call them honest. But to use the sick irony of hiding behind a charity? I don't know what you'd call that."

My mind, still in the grips of the hullaballoo that transpired in the city tonight, not to mention vodka, takes a moment to assess what he's getting at. However, once I do, and I find the connection between the two key pieces, the people I'm working for and a charity, understanding comes to me like a cold-handed slap across the face.

At the raid earlier, Igor weaseled out of an arrest with that charity stratagem. My dad knows I was there tonight. He knows I'm part of it. He knows I'm employed by people who rob, intimidate, and murder.

"I don't know what you're talking about," I say, reflexively using lying as a last-ditch defense against this surprisingly accurate accusation.

"Sit down," he says.

"It's late. I have to go to bed." I cut my eye contact from him and begin pacing toward the steps.

He bounds out of the armchair and clamps his hands around my shoulders. With a grunt, he throws me onto the couch. "Sit the fuck down," he shouts, his voice booming through the house.

As I lie there, catching my breath, I hear the master-bedroom door open upstairs. He must've woken up my mom.

"When you took that job at the limousine company," he says, "I wanted to make sure you were at a good place, with good people. So I had my guys look into the firm. The owner, Barney Hobkins, has a record. Nothing major, but still, a record. But I didn't say a thing. You were out of college, you were your own man. And you liked it there. I trusted you could take care of yourself. Then, a couple weeks ago, when you left your phone on the couch and I took it to you, while I'm driving with it in my cup holder I see a text show up on the screen from Barney Hobkins. A pickup address, a drop-off address, and a password. Sure, it could've been legitimate, part of a ride for a corporate client who requires some sort of password. But, you told me you weren't working that night. You told me you were going to a bar. So I called a detective buddy of mine in the NYPD. I told him to drive by the addresses and check things out. I was sure he'd tell me it was just a false alarm. But instead, he tells me he spots a handful of persons of interest tied to the Russian mafia. He tells me he thinks something fishy is going on, tells me he's going to investigate. And he did. And he may not have found legal evidence to convince a judge of anything tonight, Brian. But what he found was enough to convince me. Convince me that I have no idea who I raised as a son."

My mother, her hands knotting the belt of her robe, her face knotted with confused stress, appears under the entryway to the den. A couple moments later, shirtless in pajama pants, so does my brother Kip.

The instant I see him, an overpowering urge tells me to blame it all on him. To tell my dad that Kip was really the one who fucked up, dealing drugs and owing gangbangers eighteen grand. To explain that I was only trying to help, that I wanted nothing to do with any of this personally.

My bottom jaw lowers and the breath in my lungs is about to sound off on all of this. However, another urge in me, a slightly more powerful one, stops it.

The expression on my dad's face, carved with shame, signals that he's had enough. His first-born has let him down by freefalling into the underworld. What would happen to his already-fractured spirit if I then told him his second-born is below in the underworld too? My father doesn't deserve that. He's been too good to both of us to deserve that.

So I keep quiet on Kip's mischief and mistake. And for a while I keep quiet in general because I don't have any sort of response.

"Dad," I eventually say, my whole family staring at me. "I'm not going to lie. I...I have been involved in what you think. Am I proud of it? No, not at all. But I had my reasons, I want you to know. I had my reasons."

"You can keep your reasons under someone else's roof. I want you out of here by the morning." My mother explodes into tears as my father retires under the archway toward the steps.

Ten

"What about him?" Samantha asks, signaling with her toe toward a man on the street eight stories beneath us.

Studying him navigate the sidewalk, I take in the choppiness of his excitable steps. "Family man," I say. "If he were single he would've spent more time combing his hair. Lawyer probably. Nice suit, but no flash. Not a defense attorney. Mergers and acquisitions. He's walking all jumpy because he just had the spicy clams at Raul's and they didn't hit him until he left, a block or so back."

She giggles, then gazes at the fellow as he winds around the corner with a slight wobble to his shoulders. Her legs, their contour brought out by the black leggings wrapped around them, dangle off the roof of her dormitory, the heel of her left sneaker softly bouncing off the brick facade every few seconds.

This last week, since I was thrown out of my home, I've been crashing at Dusty's, but spending time at Samantha's too. He knows the whole story about my dad, but she nothing. She's a nice girl from a nice family. Telling her my brother has a gangland target on his back for a botched coke sale could scare her off. Telling her I've been driving night shifts for an illegal casino to help could only make her run faster as she left.

So I've been lying. Christmas, for instance, which was last Monday, I told her I spent eating roasted turkey and frosted cookies in Dingan with my entire family, where in reality I spent it with Dusty and a delivery pizza.

The hardest part of my lying to her is the hiding of my emotions. The image of my dad's shamed face in the den hasn't left my brain, and it seems to have leaked into my entire central nervous system, affecting every feeling and sensation I've had since, making the good a little less good and the bad a lot more bad.

Thank God I have Samantha. If the excitement of this new relationship weren't in my life during this down period, I may not have the juice to even get out of bed in the morning. I've never liked a girl more. And she likes me back. She's beautiful and sweet and smart and she likes me back.

I've been doing a lot of thinking this last week and find it odd how I've gained such a great thing the exact same time I lost another. I have this budding romance with Samantha, yet lost the long-built respect of my father.

This is no coincidence. They're related. If life had been progressing according to convention, how it's been the last decade, things would be reversed, my relationship with my father intact, mine with Samantha non-existent. But since Dusty introduced me to a world outside of convention, I decided to commit acts that pushed away my dad, while deciding to talk to out-of-my-league Samantha at the bar that night, two things foreign to the old me.

I'm still not sure what to make of this realization. I know it's important. But I don't know what to do with it.

The last half hour Samantha and I've been up here on her roof, shooting the shit and sharing our guesses about the lives of the showcase of New Yorkers on the street below, something we've done before that we both enjoy.

"I'll give you that he was a family man," she says. "But I don't think he was antsy from anything he *ate*." She tugs at the bottom of her gray sweater. "Did you see his shirt?"

"What about it?" I ask, sitting about a foot behind her and a foot to her right on a beach chair with a frame rusted brown and fabric riddled with blotches, a stack of five or six of these old, neon-colored seats up on the roof at all times, grandfathered down from NYU students of the early 2000s likely.

"The front of his shirt was *untucked*," she says with a smirk. "Just a tad. A key clue you missed. He wasn't at a restaurant. He was at a strip club. There's a real seedy one four blocks down." She pats her blond locks. "Explains why the hair was so messy too."

With a lift of her chin and a lean of her head she delivers me a look of self-satisfaction, then turns her attention toward the city skyline, which is caressed by a reddish-orange backdrop as the sun sets, boxed between the silhouettes of two rooftop water towers in the distance.

"All right, you win that one," I say. "But I definitely had you beat on the lady with the three poodles." Both her legs swaying over the ledge, she sarcastically huffs. "I can play this game all day," I go on. "There are a ton of characters in this town."

"Isn't it funny?" she asks, her focus on the foot traffic eight levels lower. "How all of them, every last one of them, have somewhere to go. And to them, getting there is more important in the moment than anything in the world."

"All of who?"

"All the people in New York. The millions on the streets and in the trains that we all take for granted, as just scenery of the city, as we go along with our day. But every one of them has a story. A place they're going. A place they need to be. Even the vagrants, the most dismissed group of all, are going from point A to point B for a *reason*. The hope of a better meal, a warmer place to sleep. Whatever it may be. To them, in that moment, the city, the whole world for that matter, is only about that."

Within my partial view of her right profile I notice her expression, which had been playful the last few minutes, bend into something else, something intense and introspective yet softened by another element I can't quite put my finger on. A sadness, above anything.

She holds this look for about ten seconds, then says, "When you're a kid they teach you to keep away from random strangers. Teachers and everyone else have you convinced they're all evil pedophiles. But after being here for a couple years, away from sheltered, suburban Long Island, I'd say that's anything but true. All these people, these random strangers, are just like us. They have wants and fears and hopes and regrets. Everyone, when you get to the root of it, is just like everyone."

Leaning toward the ledge, I glimpse the dozens of bustling bodies under us, then glue my attention to the horizon, where a patch of stormy clouds rises as the sun falls.

Samantha turns to me after a couple seconds, her expression restored to its playful state. "I'm hungry," she says, then grips my thigh and shakes it, the beach chair shaking with me. "Let's order in. Chinese?"

We make it down to her dorm room, but neither makes it to the phone. I kiss her and she kisses back. I lean onto the bed and she leans back. Soon our clothes are off. And for the first time, we have sex.

I don't say anything when we're done. Neither does she. Not because the sex wasn't good. It was great. But because things feel so right that words would only interrupt the near-mystical peace inside this little room.

My arms tighten around her and I nuzzle in closer. I needed this right now. I need her right now. My father's weeklong contamination of my sensations disappears. For a brief moment I feel only good. A lot of good. Until the world goes away as I drift to sleep.

Eleven

"Brian." Darkness. "Hey." Spots of light. "You up?" The scent of Samantha's perfume. I blink. Things in her dorm room, through a blur, a ruffled orange pillowcase, a shaggy area rug, a Taylor Swift poster over her roommate's bed.

I blink again. I see Samantha's face. "You're up," she says with a smile. My mind is still half-asleep and I'm unable to conjure coherent thoughts, however my body is wide awake, injected with a feeling of panic.

Something is horribly wrong. I shoot up in her bed. "What's the matter?" she asks, making a funny face.

I rip the sheets off myself, roll off the mattress naked, and grope for my clothing, flung about on the floor. "What time is it?" I ask.

"Babe, what's wrong?"

"Just tell me what time it is."

Sitting cross-legged on the bed, she shoots me an expression that's one part perplexed, one part peeved, then grabs her iPhone from the night table and glimpses the screen. "Four minutes after eleven. We were passed out for a while, huh?"

My neck stiffens as its skin chills. "Shit, oh shit." I grasp my balled-up jeans, untwist them from inside out, and hastily maneuver my legs through them. "Where's my shirt?"

"I don't know."

"Help me find my shirt," I bark as I scan the room for it. Rain pounds on the windows.

"What the hell is going on, Brian?"

I pick up one of my boots, stumbling into her wall as I try to stuff my foot inside. "My shirt," I say.

As I lace up my shoes she combs through the tangle of sheets and pillows for my shirt. "Here," she says after a few moments, holding it up.

I sprint to her, snatch it, and slide it over myself, then lunge to her desk and pluck my wallet, phone, and keys from it. Checking my text messages, I see one from Barney with the details of tonight's event. It came in over two hours ago. I'm late. Much later than I was when I screwed up my first night.

"When you visit your parents in Long Island, you drive, right?" I ask her.

"Yeah, why?"

"Your car. It's in the city?"

"Yeah, why?"

"I need it."

"Now?"

Shoving my phone and wallet in my jeans, I say, "I have to drive tonight. I slept through the beginning of my shift. I don't have time to go all the way to Queens, get my limo, and come back into Manhattan."

"How are you going to go to work as a limo driver without your limo?"

"It's...it's not like that...I just...I need your car, okay?"

"Why don't you call your boss and tell him you're running a little late? I'm sure someone else can cover you for a little if—"

"They can't. It has to be me. I…it has to be me. You don't understand. Where's your car?"

She observes me with the same expression as before, part perplexed, part peeved, and I can tell she's angry. However, I'm sure she can tell I'm in trouble. And the nurturing part of her soul must tell her not to ask questions right now, just to help. Her stare cools to a look and her voice calms to a whisper as she says, "Hold on, let me get my purse."

Three minutes later we're outside in the rain, jogging toward the parking garage where she stores her Chevy Malibu.

A puddle explodes as my boot thumps it, the dirty water dampening the bottom of my jeans and dripping down my ankles, bare without the socks I left behind somewhere in the dorm room. This mess will have to be my work outfit tonight, my suit on a hanger in my Sonata back in Queens.

We're heading along Canal Street, Samantha a few strides behind me. We cross Broadway. Two-way traffic speeds by to my left, while the yellow of a "CASH FOR GOLD" sign streaks by to the right as I pass a wet jumble of tightly packed storefront awnings.

We keep going. My jacket is soaked. My shoulders shiver inside it. Glancing behind, I see Samantha, still moving but lagging. I stop, waiting for her to catch up, then take her by the hand and continue ahead at a pace she can withstand.

"Watch it," a delivery guy in a rain poncho shouts, stopping short on a bicycle in front of us, his front wheel sliding across the pavement with a screech, nearly grinding into my knees. "Look where you're fucking going," he hollers at me. I stare at him for a second, don't take the time to apologize, and run on.

Samantha's purse, held by its leather strap in her right hand, bounces up and down as we advance. In my periphery I see objects explode out of the top.

"Dammit," she yells. My momentum carries me ahead a couple steps, then I stop and turn around, noticing her on her hands and knees peeling her spilt belongings off the sidewalk. Lipstick, Advil, blush, mace, moisturizer. I rush over to help her. Crouching down across from her, I see her makeup is running, bluish-black zigzags coming down her cheeks with the rainwater. We pick everything up, stick it back in her bag, and keep moving.

After a couple more blocks, she says, "Right on Varick," winded, her voice hollow. In five minutes we reach the garage and dash through the entrance. We follow the floor as it slopes down, rain spattering from our soggy clothing onto the concrete. The surface levels and a glass booth comes into sight, inside an attendant, a Mexican kid no older than sixteen in a baggy button-down shirt.

Samantha unearths her monthly-parking card from her saturated purse and presents it to him. "Okay miss," he responds, then takes his time locating the keys of her Chevy Malibu from a pegboard.

While he tracks down her car I lean over, clutch the knees of my jeans, and inhale the polluted parking-garage oxygen, recovering from the trek. Samantha rests against a drainpipe on the wall doing the same.

Silence for a half-minute other than the sound of our breath and the swoosh of traffic outside on the street.

"Thanks," I say to her, still bent over. "I only need the car for a couple hours. I'll let you know when I'm done and bring it right back."

"You think I'm going to allow you to take my car without you telling me what you're doing with it?"

I stand, the shine of the tube lights on the ceiling shooting into my eyes. "I told you. I'm working."

"You're limo driving without a *limo*, Brian? It doesn't make sense."

Four footsteps echo through the parking structure. A couple in its seventies, arm in arm, is traversing the slope in high-end raincoats, playbills in their hands. They stop at the unmanned attendant stand, pleasantly smiling at us. Neither of us smiles back.

"What do you want me to tell you?" I ask Samantha in a hushed voice.

"What the hell you're using my car for. We were napping. Next thing I know you're wigging out. You demand to drive it. I'm nice enough to give it to you. I book it across the city with you in the rain. You at least owe me an explanation."

She's right. I do owe her an explanation. But that'd involve the truth. Something I'm not prepared to give her.

Before I can think of a believable lie, I hear the hum of an engine and see the gray nose of a Chevy Malibu roll around the corner. The attendant opens the driver's door and fixes his stare on Samantha.

Her eyes are still focused on me. "I'm coming with you," she states.

"No, you can't," I say, my heart speeding up.

"Why not?"

"I...it's not...you can't...please just—"

"What are you hiding from me?"

"Nothing. But I—"

"If you're not hiding anything, let me come with you." My mind probes its depths for a solution to this problem. It doesn't find one. She turns to the attendant and says, "Sir, please do not let this man in my car unless I say it's okay." Then she peers at me. The old couple does too. "Well?"

I check my phone. Already past eleven thirty, a pile of passengers likely waiting for me pissed off in the rain. If I fuck this up and Igor fires me, my brother won't get his money and my fallout with my dad would be for nothing. Each additional minute that passes, the likelier this'll be my fate.

I squeeze my eyelids tight. "Fine," I tell her, at a loss for another option. "Get in."

Soon we zoom up the incline to Varick Street, the rain slapping the windshield once we exit the garage. Samantha doesn't sit normally, with her knees pointed ahead, but cross-legged, as she did in the bed, her body facing me. Her eyes are cold with doubt, watching my every move, waiting for me to reveal myself as someone I'm not.

We go a block. Then another. Silence. I flip on the radio hoping a third-party distraction could cut some of the tension, however it just makes the small space we share more uncomfortable than it already is, an annoying commercial on the air for an appliance store, a sound effect of a bomb going off every few seconds along with a singsongy voice heralding, "We're blowing up prices at Boomer's."

A car honks at me as I cut it off, through its windshield a hazy image of the driver giving me the bird. I fly along 6th Avenue by Washington Square Park, my tires blasting a wave of rainwater onto the sidewalk.

Charink. My head bobs down then up as a wheel nails a pothole. Not wearing a seatbelt, Samantha rocks toward the glove box, putting her hand out for support. I feel her gaze on me without actually seeing it as she buckles up.

Approaching my pickup destination, Madison and East 63rd, I wrestle with how I'm going to do the job effectively without letting on to its illegality.

I notice about a dozen opened umbrellas huddled at the intersection, among them men and women with their jackets slung over their heads as shields from the weather. The gamblers. There's a backup of over twenty.

Stomping the gas, I speed through a yellow light, then screech to a halt in front of the ritzy jewelry store on the corner.

Apoplectic eyes peer at me through the wet shadows under the umbrellas. I open the door and step into the damp night. As the rain strikes me I say to the group, "I'm sorry I'm late but—"

"I've been standing out here for a goddamn hour," one of the men shouts.

"I apologize. But I'm here now. And I want to get you all there, out of the rain. The four who've been waiting the longest, come with me now."

"Get in where?" a woman asks, throwing up her hands, her Louis Vuitton bag swinging about her shoulder.

I drum the hood of the Malibu, drops of cold water on it splashing up my sleeve, chilling my arm. "I had engine trouble with my limo. I'll bring you there in this. Come on."

Waving them toward me, I dive back into the car. As I shift it into drive I catch Samantha's stare. She looks at me in a way she never has before, as a stranger.

Unable to bear the image, I turn ahead. I swallow, realizing how dry the inside of my throat is, an odd sensation paired with the wetness on its outside.

The back door opens. In the rearview I see umbrellas, briefcases, coats, ties, and earrings, everything drenched. Four bodies wiggle into the back. Grumbles waft forward. Finally, the door closes. I push the pedal, embarking toward 5th and Central Park South.

"Who the hell is she?" a gritty male voice asks. Twisting my head behind, I see a fiftyish man with a deep widow's peak glaring at Samantha.

"Who the hell are *you*?" she asks him back.

"I'm the client. So are these people next to me. And he's the driver. And in this car, at any time, there should only be clients and one driver. So please, dear, kindly tell me where you fit in."

She doesn't answer.

"Is this your girlfriend?" the gritty voice scoffs in my direction. "You told your girlfriend about everything?"

"My limo had engine problems," I blurt. "And I...I needed to borrow her car. That's all. She doesn't know anything."

"I don't know anything about *what*?" Samantha asks.

"Jesus fucking Christ," the man with the widow's peak says as he sinks into his seat. He lets out a contemptuous laugh.

"*What* don't I know about, Brian?" Samantha asks, her voice louder now.

We hit a stretch of traffic, coasting to a standstill. I look at the clock. Heat from six close-together bodies permeates the interior. I see Samantha's angry eyes in my periphery, see my sweaty forehead in the rearview mixed in with the reflections of livid passengers. We crawl toward the apartment complex, the temperature of the car heating up each block.

Finally we get there, a luxury high-rise with bull's-eye windows overlooking Central Park. The passengers exit. On his way to the entrance the guy with the widow's peak stops in the beam of my headlights. He holds a dirty look on me for a few seconds, then continues on.

"Brian," Samantha says, shutting off the radio. "Be honest with me dammit. Who were those people?"

"I'll explain," I say reflexively, though I have no intention to.

"Then explain."

I'm silent. I'll think of something to say, a way out of this, once I complete the pickups and my mind is clear again. I just need to hold out until then.

She interrogates me the whole way back to Madison and East 63rd. I don't satisfy her with my evasive answers. I don't even look at her. But what else am I supposed to do?

I get out and direct the next four passengers in, while telling a newly arrived pair that things are a bit pushed back tonight.

In a short while I stop in front of the building overlooking Central Park. "Enjoy your evening," I tell them. As they get out, in my headlights, once again, I notice the guy with the widow's peak. He's on the sidewalk pointing at me, his mouth moving. Another man stands to his right.

Igor.

I tap my fingers on the edge of Samantha's steering wheel. I hold my breath. Soon the short, stout frame of my former passenger drifts away, toward the building's door, leaving only Igor out here.

My fingers are still in motion, my breath still on pause. He takes a few steps forward, into the rain, the features of his face emerging from the canopy's shadow. I gulp, the dry interior of my throat scraping against itself.

He comes to the curb, a couple feet from the passenger-side window.

Samantha eyes him through the damp glass, then turns to me. He extends his manicured hand to the back door and opens it, the interior lights of the Malibu springing on. The sound of rain intensifies inside the open car. I haven't had a breath since I spotted him. Among all this wetness it feels like I'm drowning.

He sits in the backseat. He shuts the door. He doesn't speak. Ten seconds pass. Twenty. Thirty.

"I…I'm sorry sir," I say. "I had engine trouble with my limo. I did whatever I could to get here. This was the only way. I'm so sorry. It's my own fault."

He's still without words. I peek at the rearview mirror to assess his reaction. There is none, his hands on his knees, his eyes on the rain outside the window. "I still have more pick-ups," I say. "I don't want to leave them waiting. Can I go get them? You're welcome to ride along if you'd like. We can—"

"No need. I sent another driver for them."

"I can get them. Please—"

"You've done enough damage already."

Silence.

"Brian, what's going on?" Samantha asks, her voice stripped of the defiance it's had since the beginning of the car ride, now touched with something more delicate, something scared.

"I'll tell you what's going on," Igor says, leaning forward, his face entering the space between my seat and Samantha's. "Your boyfriend is a fool. That's what's going on."

She swallows, scopes me, then him. "And what are you to him?" she asks Igor.

"Honey, please don't," I say, laying my hand atop hers.

"You can both get out of my car right now if neither of you explains this to me."

"Brian," Igor says, his focus on Samantha, his face only inches from hers. "Do yourself a favor and shut this cunt up."

I watch her bottom lip drop and her eyebrows rise. A gasp. A gaze in my direction. Another in Igor's. Another in mine. She waits for me to do something, to defend her. And I know I should.

But I don't. I'm too scared.

She turns from me back to him and yells, "Get the hell out of my car," brazen in her ignorance that he's a mobster with a reputation for disconnecting thumbs from the bodies they were born on. "Out, *now*."

He smirks. "Brian, are you going to shut her up, or am I?"

"Out," she screams, then pushes his shoulder.

His brow creases and his eyelids tighten. He stares her down, swings his hand back, and slaps her in the mouth.

The skin-on-skin cracking noise is quick and loud, almost like a gunshot. Samantha's face leaves my view, hidden behind her blond locks which are still quivering from the recoil of her head upon impact.

I feel my body shrinking in the driver's seat, while the emotions inside it grow. I'm six inches tall, yet the rage, regret, and repulsion in me are a mile wide, stretching me, splitting me apart.

She bursts out of the car and runs. I get out and run after her. If I caught up to her I wouldn't even know what to say. But still, I run.

After a few blocks the image of her is lost in the rain. She's gone. The only great thing I had left in this world is gone.

Twelve

I wander through Central Park. I'm not going anywhere, and I don't remember how I even got here. After I lost Samantha on the street I just started walking. I figured it'd help keep me sane. It isn't working.

The rain quieted a bit but it's not exactly clear, the atmosphere stuffed with a motionless mist. With my head down I travel along a pavement pathway, the slick surface appearing like a black sheet of ice, the cold moisture in the air clinging to the back of my neck as I wind deeper into the wooded interior of the park.

Soon I cross a bridge and the city's skyscrapers are cropped from view, replaced by a thicket of bare tree branches extending upward and inward. Three pigeons ahead on the walkway look at me for a second, flap their wings, and lift toward the blackish-gray sky.

I'm now alone. No buildings, no animals, no people. But my mind isn't. It's filled with everything I've lost. Of course, my relationship with Samantha. And also, the capability to protect my brother.

I can't go on driving for Igor, not after what he did. Even if he accepted me, I couldn't do it. My soul, which has been gradually bent since I took this job, has its breaking point.

And I'd bust through it for groveling back to that monster for money, something I could never forgive myself for.

Which means my brother will fall short on his debt. And he'll be forced to ask my dad for the remainder, disclosing the coke predicament. My father will soon realize not just one, but both of his sons have failed him. We'll become unrecognizable to him and he'll become unrecognizable to himself. And I'll be responsible.

When my brother approached me for help, I should've been more practical. Convincing him to go to my dad from the beginning would've been infinitely better than this. That way, the downside would've been the revelation that just one of his children was a fuck-up. But because of my hasty older-brother advice, he'll soon know we both are.

I trudge deeper into the woods, farther from the world.

And I stay there most of the night, just walking around. Often I think of Igor. And how much I want to hurt him, how much I want to get him back for what he did to Samantha.

But the thousand times I experience the thought, a thousand times I experience disappointment. I know it'd be a suicide mission to take a swing at him. Sure, filled with rage, maybe I could edge him out in a fight despite the size difference. However, after it was done, after I left, it'd only be a matter of time. Until he, or one of his countless trained goons, snuck up behind me one day. Maybe with a piano wire around my throat. Maybe with an injection of poison in my arm. Maybe with a bullet to the head.

Definitely, one way or another, I wouldn't get out alive.

My phone dead, I hail a cab and ride it back to Big Hitter, where my Sonata's been parked.

The teeth of regret sink deeper into me once I see it. I wanted to hang out with Samantha before my shift. And I knew Big Hitter wouldn't reimburse me if I parked the Sonata in a garage by her dorm, since that'd be a personal, not business, expense. So I opted for the slightly cheaper option of stashing it for free in the Big Hitter lot and taking an Uber to her building.

If I just paid the few extra bucks and put it in a garage, I would've used my own nearby car to do the pickups after waking from the nap. No need for Samantha's Malibu. No Samantha coming on the trip. No Igor smacking her.

I make the drive back to Dusty's place in Pramin, the purplish orange of a winter dawn swelling outside the windows. I park behind his Jeep and open the cabin's door with the spare key he gave me last weekend.

When I enter I expect a sleepy house, expect Dusty in bed. But there he is, under the all-on lights, at the kitchen table he made with his own hands, a pot of coffee and a mug at his side, a crazed look in his eyes.

He peers at me and says, "Let's hit this bastard where it hurts."

Thirteen

"What the hell are you doing awake?" I ask.

"Let's take a walk."

"Where?"

He chugs the remaining coffee in his mug, gets up, and trots out the front door. Following him outside, I cross the grass of his lawn, which glistens with early-morning frost, and hustle to his side.

"What is this about?" I ask.

"I told you already," he says, stepping onto his street, Lantern Lane, a dirt road mostly bordered by boulders and trees, the homes long distances apart. "We need to hit him."

"Who?"

"Igor. I know what he did."

"How…wait…*how*?"

"When I got up to the event, people were talking about you. Said you showed up to do your runs in your girlfriend's Chevy. Igor got pissed and went downstairs. I was worried about you, so kept peeking through the curtains down at the building entrance. I saw what happened. That scumbag hit your girl. Now we hit him."

I laugh at the lunacy of this idea, which I've already had a thousand times roaming Central Park. "You don't think I wanted to slug him after I saw what he did to her? He'd kill us."

The cold air burrows under my coat, into my torso, and I wince. Dusty, like usual, isn't fazed by the weather.

"You're right," he says. "He probably would kill us if we tried to punch him." He stops walking. So do I. "That's why we're going to hit him in a different way. A smarter way. That'll hurt him much more than any punch." He brushes some dirty-blond hair from his eyes, which harbor a look more crazed than the one from inside.

"What kind of way?" I say.

"What's the one thing Igor cares about more than anything?" he asks, walking again, our bodies sloping up and down over one of the road's many humps.

"Not getting busted by the cops?"

"True, that's important," he says. "But he can slither out of legal trouble. He can pay cops off. Think deeper. What would the cops be busting him for in the first place? What's the one thing that makes a New York casino illegal?"

"The house making money."

"Bingo." Dusty faces me as we stride, a trace of teeth appearing between his lips, which soon spread into a smile. "It's Igor's job to make sure the casino earns a certain amount of dough at each event. He's responsible for the bottom line. And the bottom line depends on how many people show up each week to gamble. After the police raid, attendance last night was about a third of what it usually is. Can you imagine what'll happen to those numbers if there's *another* evacuation?"

"Yeah, they'll drop. And he'll hate it. But what are you suggesting? We secretly call the cops on him during the next event? With us inside? If they start snooping around and find something incriminating on him, we'll get dragged into the station too. And believe me, my dad won't use any of his connections to help us out. In fact, he'll tell his detective friend to go harder on us just to make a point."

"You're right. The cops are the last people we'll want there the night this goes down. But for a different reason."

"What do you mean?"

"We won't want the cops there because you and I are going to rob the casino."

An auburn ball of sun slowly ascends behind him among the shadowed tree branches.

It takes me about ten seconds to fully absorb what he said, and another ten to closely inspect his expression for hints of sarcasm. Finding none, I ask, "Have you gone mad?"

His eyes go wide, the bright blue centers loud against the gray sky behind him. "Maybe just a little."

"I need to get some sleep," I say, then turn my back to him and troop back toward the cabin. I hear the bop of his boots behind me. Then feel his hand on my shoulder. He spins me around. I push him away. "No, Dusty. *No*. Are you kidding me? Really? Why the fuck would we rob the casino?"

"Do you want to keep working for that asshole after what he did to Samantha?"

"Of course not...but...how—"

"Well, neither do I. But I still want enough money to travel the world. And I know you need more money to help out your brother. I've been thinking about this *all* night. I have it figured out. You and I'll walk away with way more cash than we both need. *And* we'll scare off gamblers, permanently hurting Igor's bottom line, giving him the payback he deserves for what he did."

"Making money and fucking over Igor sounds great, Dusty. It really does. But how the hell are you going to pull off a magic trick like stealing from a mafia casino? Dozens of people are walking around those apartments. Almost all of them know us. Especially you. Not to mention, the safe with the money is sitting right next to Zlata the cashier and an armed guard all night."

"That's where the evacuation comes into play. We call in a fake police scare. And just like last week, chaos breaks out. That's our time to act."

I let out a long breath. Through my head buzzes the gamut of possible dangers with Dusty's proposal. One screams at me stronger than the rest. "Distracting the crowd and getting to the safe would be hard enough," I say. "Really hard. Almost-impossible hard. Let's pretend for whatever reason you get lucky and do it. You'd still be on *camera*. They're all over the place. One is *always* on the cashier area."

Grinning, he reaches into his pocket. "The camera won't be a problem." Pulling his hand out, he reveals a shiny, cylindrical object. I take a step closer to check it out, still unsure what it is. He aims it at a tree and clicks a button on it, a red dot flashing on the bark. "Any simple, drugstore laser pointer, just like this, can knock out the camera for us."

He passes it to me. I roll it around in my fingers, chapped from my rove around Central Park.

"Remember I told you I worked as a bar-back in New Orleans?" he asks. "My first job when I got to town was at this place in the French Quarter called Dugan Blues. Thursdays were our big day. All the employees knew there was a ton of loot in the registers on Thursday. At the end of a night, during Mardi Gras when we did the most business, the boss notices we're short. Short a lot. So he looks at the tapes from the security cameras. For a ten-minute stretch the recording from the camera on the cash registers turns all funky. It's just blobs of red and yellow light. So he takes the tape to the New Orleans Police Department. And the detective knew right away. Said it was a laser pointer. According to him, if you shine one into a camera, the sensor in the lens can't handle the brightness. It...overloads it in a way."

Hands on his hips he analyzes my expression, attempting to gauge my reaction. Two emotions, excitement and apprehension, wage war on the battlefield of my face, my lips fluttering into a grin then quickly flinging into firmness, my eyes springing open then quickly settling to a squint.

It's a lot to take, so I sit on a roadside rock. Dusty descends on the one next to mine.

He's clearly put a lot of thought into this. And the potential rewards are nothing short of stupendous. If we got access to that safe I could walk away with enough money to not only rescue my brother and avoid him having to expose his situation to my dad, but steer my own destiny. I could start my own business. Do something I love. Set myself up for the rest of my life.

Equally enticing is the bottom-line justice for Igor. I felt so damn small and powerless when he whacked Samantha, and I sat there too petrified to act. Even if she never speaks to me again, which she probably won't, I could become whole again if I knew I did something to avenge the assault on her.

However, the downside to all this is death. No question about it. If we get caught, we get killed.

The old Brian surely would've proceeded down the conventional route. The one where he doesn't rob the mafia casino. However, after all I've been through the last few weeks, the more I realize the unconventional path, though scarier, often is the better choice in life. But only if you tread it in a sensible way.

So I decide to entertain Dusty's proposal. Though I won't go through with it unless he gives me every detail, and every detail gives me airtight assurance.

"Tell me more about how we'd get inside the safe," I say.

He grins, elated that he's hooked me. "We're going nowhere near the safe. Too risky."

"How're we going to get the money without getting to the safe?"

"We're not getting the money. We're getting *chips*."

"We're not allowed to gamble at events. We can't cash in chips."

"I know. That's why we're not going to cash them in."

Fourteen

Dusty and I stare up at the facade of the three-story town-house owned by Vince Berrini, the poker player we had a drink with after the NYPD raid then dropped off at this very home. Dusty clacks the knocker.

The door soon opens, revealing Vince in a green bath-robe, a V-shaped patch of chest skin showing, flesh of the same color and texture exposed on his shins. Puzzlement glints in his eyes. "Boys," he says. "To what do I owe the pleasure?"

A few minutes later Dusty and I are on the couch in the den, Vince in a chair across, light spilling in from the court-yard, shining on shelves of framed photos which feature him posing with various big shots. Senators, Las Vegas hotel magnates, NFL players. On the TV plays the Ingmar Bergman movie *Wild Strawberries*.

"What if I told you I could sell you poker chips for eighty cents on the dollar?" Dusty asks him.

Vince buries his fingers into a bag of microwaved popcorn tucked beside him in the chair, comes out with a handful, and tosses it in his mouth. "What sort of poker chips?" he asks as he chews.

"The kind you've been using to gamble in the penthouses."

Vince jiggles the bag, the un-popped kernels at the bottom rattling around. "How'd you get your hands on those?"

"Hypothetically...if, for whatever reason, Brian and I happened to come across some of them, would you be willing to buy them from us for eighty cents on the dollar?"

Vince rests his elbows on his knees and cups his hands together, the polka-dot pattern of his boxer shorts showing beneath the robe. He examines Dusty's face for a second, then mine, and asks, "What the hell are you two up to?"

"The details don't matter," Dusty says. "We came here to make you a business proposition. You're a successful businessman. The deal should be a no-brainer. Buy chips from us at four-fifths their value, and cash them in at the next event for full price. You make a twenty-percent profit in an instant."

"Twenty-five-percent profit," I correct.

"Twenty-five," Dusty says, his voice loudening on "five."

Vince stands. He begins pacing back and forth across the den's fractal-patterned area rug. "Please don't tell me you're going to steal anything from Igor," he says mid-stride. "Please tell me you're both not that dumb."

In a soothing tone, Dusty says, "All we're asking *you* to do is something *smart*. Collect a twenty-five-percent profit without doing a thing."

"I've been playing in underground dens for decades. I've seen people try all sorts of shenanigans before. They never work. Trust me. You—"

"It's not—"

"Don't interrupt me, dammit," Vince says, wagging his finger at Dusty, the motion causing the belt of his robe to loosen, the flaps creeping apart. Re-knotting it, he says, "It's a fucking death wish, you understand?"

"Don't worry about us." Dusty surfaces that easy smile of his, one I've seen so many times before, one that coolly promises you that everything, for one reason or another, even if you don't know it yet, will be okay.

"You fucking guarantee me you've got this under control, Dusty?" Vince asks.

"Guaranteed."

Vince grips the back of his chair, a crisscross of creases forming on the cushy fabric. His eyes slant upward. "Igor's bound to eventually see a discrepancy in his books if chips go missing."

"Sure," Dusty says. "*Eventually*. We think we can get about a hundred grand of them. Millions upon millions of dollars go through that casino. Nobody will notice a hundred-thousand-dollar gap right away. There are way too many chips in circulation for that. The next time they do a full-on analysis of the financial records they'll catch it. But by then the deal will be done. We can get the chips to you this week, right after the event. You cash them in the following week for your profit. At that point the three of us are removed from it. Down the road, when Igor finds out some went missing, it won't be your problem. Or ours." Dusty smirks. "It'll be his."

Vince lets out a long exhale and lets go of the chair. His eyes slant back down, focusing on us. His head slowly flows into a nod. "All right. I'll fucking do it."

"That's my man," Dusty says, popping up from the sofa. He shakes Vince's hand and slaps his back.

My face tingles. The fantasy has just turned into a reality.

A few hours later in Pramin, a stack of chips erupts as my hand tries to clutch it, a couple sliding through the slit between my index and middle finger, three plummeting to the floor, wobbling, pausing at my feet.

"Shit," I scream.

"You didn't get the grab but the speed improved," Dusty says, glancing at a stopwatch from the corner of his garage workshop.

This morning we converted it to a practice area for the chip heist we have planned for Saturday. We pushed the woodworking supplies against the wall and used the floor space to create a small-scale model of a typical casino event, with pieces of scrap lumber representing common features in their common arrangements, duct-tape-and-marker labels on each, "Blackjack Tables," "Roulette Tables," "Craps Tables," "Poker Tables," "Bar," "Cashier Area," "Elevator," "Stairwell."

I bend over and pluck the spilt chips off the concrete floor, my oversized topcoat, drooping and dangling, getting in my way. At Walmart this morning, in addition to the stopwatch and rack of poker chips, we bought an extra-large topcoat, burlap sack, and sewing kit, then stitched the sack to the lining of the jacket. The idea is that once I snatch the chips on Saturday I'll dump them inside the bag. Its depth combined with the coat's loose fit wouldn't cause a suspicious protrusion, letting me sneak out during the evacuation without piquing anyone's attention.

However, none of that matters if I can't cleanly make the grab from the cashier rack in the first place, something I've been struggling with all afternoon.

"Ready to go again?" Dusty asks.

I take a deep breath. "I guess."

He clicks a few buttons on the stopwatch. "All right. And... *now.*"

I dash toward the workbench, where the poker rack rests, and using my thumb, index, and middle fingers, like a claw, clamp chips in clumps of five, rifle them inside the bag in my coat, and repeat. Fifteen inside. Twenty. New column. Twenty-five. Thirty. *Bumt*, *hish*, *klink*, *klenk*, *klonk*. Five spilt chips spin at my feet. "Fuck," I shout, kicking the leg of the workbench.

"You're getting better," Dusty says.

"Great, I went from really shitty to just somewhat shitty. I still can't do it."

"It's just the nerves getting in the way."

"No it's not. It's hard."

"You're making it harder than it really is."

"Easy for you to say. All you need to do is flash a light." Since Dusty has a better sense for the people at the event and is a couple inches taller than me, with a longer reach, we decided it'd be best if he took care of shining the laser pointer within the crowd, while I grabbed the chips.

"Let's try it again," he says with a clap. "C'mon."

I pace around the workshop, my dirty sneaker soles imprinting pieces of labeled lumber on the floor. The cranked-up space heater, heavy topcoat, and incessant chip fumbling produce a steamy, swampy sensation on my skin.

"I don't want to try it again," I tell him.

"What do you mean?"

"I want...I have...let's just take a break, all right?" I sit on the concrete, the long, black jacket extending over piles of wood shavings from Dusty's furniture whittling. Objects in the workshop start spinning, screwdrivers and paintbrushes, containers of wood stain and paint thinner. I run my fingers through my hair, the heel of my hand rubbing against my feverish forehead. Maybe Dusty is right. Maybe my nerves are getting to me. Maybe the reality of what we're going to do, rob the Russian mob, is too much for me to bear.

He sits beside me, his elbows mounted on his knees. We don't speak for fifteen or so seconds. "She'd be honored, you know?" he says.

"Who?"

"Samantha. If she knew what you were putting yourself through. To make things right. To get back at Igor. She doesn't know any of it, does she?"

I shake my head.

"Well," he says, "if she did...she probably would do everything to stop you from going through with it. But still...she'd be honored...that you wanted to do it. For her."

"Hopefully."

"Hey, I've got an idea. Let's see how things work with the roles flipped. I'll grab the chips, you take out the camera."

"You sure?"

"Can't hurt to try it. Think you'd be able to manage shining the laser pointer in the middle of the crowd?"

"A lot of the men are taller than me, but…if I got the right angle…yeah, well…maybe."

"One thing at a time. Let's see how I do with the chips. Then we can practice with the laser. Cool?"

"Cool."

Looking at his exuberant face, I remind myself that he hardly knows Samantha. It seems bizarre that he's amped up enough to risk his life to enact revenge for her.

But then I remember the story he told me in this very garage about his mother. This isn't just about Samantha. It's about his father and every other asshole who's hit a woman. It's about cosmic justice for him. Not to mention, the money. Half of a hundred grand, even with the cut for Vince, is enough money to cross the globe multiple times.

He'd live his dream. A woodworking world traveler. Nothing more. Nothing less. Dusty Walnen. A woodworking world traveler.

I like how this isn't just about me. How we're each doing this for personal reasons equally as powerful. And there's nobody I'd rather have on my side during something as crazily unconventional as this than Dusty.

He takes the black topcoat from me, slips it on, and says, "According to Vince, nobody pulls stuff like this off. Well Brian, let's make some history then."

Fifteen

Steept, steept, steept. My limo's left windshield wiper has a slight kink in the rubber, squeaking against the icy glass each time it comes down. It's been snowing for three hours or so and the roads are starting to slicken.

My ears are tuned into the soft sound because I'm not conversing with my passengers. Tonight, the night Dusty and I are going to rob the Russian mafia, small talk is no priority.

After a phony apology to Igor, and a load of pleading to Barney, I was allowed back as a casino driver. Apparently, following the NYPD raid, two of the other drivers got jittery and quit. Understaffed, they needed me. So here I am.

My final pickup is in the backseat. In a matter of minutes I'll be in the casino. In a matter of an hour a fake scare about the cops will be in play. And a bit after that a bag of gold chips, worth a grand each, will be in our hands.

The quiet outside accentuates the silence in the limo, not many other cars on the road in this weather and at this hour even in the heart of Chelsea.

Snowflakes dancing in my headlight beams, I make the drop-off at the building, near the corner of 5th and West 21st, then park. I trek on foot along 6th Avenue, my hands docked in my pockets. Thick snow chunks creep through the back of my collar, streams of icy water snaking down the length of my spine to the top of my underwear, the nerve endings in my torso rigid.

My nose is consumed by the smell of honey-roasted nuts from a vendor's cart. The warm scent cuts through the cold air even from almost a block away. It reminds me of Samantha. After our first date, lunch in Little Italy, we took a walk and stopped at one of these stands.

I finally make it to the building, called Tyche Place, emblazoned in bronze letters on one of the front stones. Entering, I step on a rug in the lobby with a large "T" sewn on it, globs of snow from the soles of my dress shoes falling off and melting on the blue nylon, aided by the vents overhead blasting heat on full dial.

As I walk across the carpet, the laser pointer in my jacket pocket grazes the top of my thigh. A nervous sweat begins beading on the skin over my spine, blending with the snowy dampness on the band of my underpants.

I get in the elevator. The ride to the twenty-second story feels like an hour. In reality it's probably just a minute, but anxiety is starting to meddle with my brain and muddle my sense of things. My hands look a smidge smaller than they usually do and my eyes, which I see in the reflection of the glass walls, look a bit bigger.

The elevator stops at the penthouse. "Mariachi," I tell the guard, providing the password. Stepping into the foyer, I notice black velvet blankets hanging on the walls, covering every inch, which I at first think is some odd decorative statement, but then I reason the apartment probably lacks curtains, its walls all glass to take advantage of a panoramic view from twenty-two stories up, and the staff needed to improvise tonight to keep the NYPD from snooping. The velvet sheets reflect the overhead light in such a way that a sheen appears on them, reminding me of the black ice on the road outside.

Let's get down to business. Step one, locate the cashier security camera.

While the band begins playing "Down to the Waterline" by the Dire Straits I create a path through the crowd, searching for the cashier station, waving to a couple of my former passengers along the way. A pack of gamblers, each holding a briefcase, protrudes from a hallway. Zlata and her supply of chips must be in a room ahead.

Sure enough, I see her at a desk in a space that must be the home's library, an eight-deck bookshelf behind her. The archway into this room is low, part of the interior obscured, the whole of the camera hidden.

Shit. This can't work unless I know exactly where it's mounted and map out an angle for the laser pointer.

The sweat on the small of my back builds. I need to get up to Zlata for a closer look. My mind scrambles for a way to do that without seeming shady. I decide to ask her a question, any question, as an excuse to get near the camera.

I stand at the tail of the line. Looking through the glasses resting on the tip of her hooked nose, an analytical expression on her face, Zlata reaches to a smorgasbord of racked chips on the desk, their colors bright against the dark blankets on the walls, peels a few dozen off, and slides them toward the first gambler ahead.

Staring at all the gold chips in the tray, I think how *these* are the ones, the actual chips that will be in the burlap bag stitched to Dusty's jacket, forty-millimeter-diameter circles of plastic soon to be responsible for a forty-thousand-dollar infusion to my net worth.

My pulse speeds up. My nervous system is intoxicated from a powerful cocktail of emotion, the excitement of tonight's opportunity laced with the terror of failing. I take a few deep breaths as I advance on the line.

In about five minutes the man in the herringbone suit who's been in front of me gets his chips and departs for the tables, putting me face to face with Zlata. Her brow crinkles in bewilderment when she sees I don't have a briefcase, deep horizontal lines running across her forehead, intersecting the network of wrinkles on her eighty-something-year-old skin. "Yes?" she asks in a rich Russian accent.

"I'm one of the drivers," I tell her. "Brian. We met once. Sorry to bother you. Did anybody turn a lost wallet into you? I think mine fell out of my coat."

She leans back in her chair, suspicion discharging from her eyes which examine me from below her jet-black bangs. "*I* haven't seen no wallet," she says, a hint of vexation in her voice as if I'm wasting her time, which technically I am.

Already she seems wary of me. If she catches me looking all over, it could tip her off that I'm up to some kind of ploy. I freeze, our gazes locked, unsure what to do, my heart bopping against my rib cage.

I take in a mouthful of air and let out a bogus cough, which gives me an excuse to shake my head. As I do I sweep my vision across the room. No sign of the camera.

I cough again. Got it, attached to the molding atop the peaked entryway into the dining room.

"Excuse me," I say as I clunk my chest with my fist. "If a wallet turns up, let me know." She holds a skeptical stare on me. Boris, the bulky guard at her side, does too. In a couple seconds she shifts her attention to the man behind me in line, motioning for him to give her his cash.

I turn and veer toward the main room, my chest varnished in sweat. I remove my jacket, drape it over the back of a chair, and sit. Still antsy, I hope I'll calm getting off my feet.

But I don't, changing positions every ten seconds or so, right leg crossed over left, left leg crossed over right, elbows on knees, hands folded, right hand on chin, fingers over mouth, fingers on cheek.

I'm not sure how much time goes by before I spot Dusty across the room. He just arrived, walking from the elevator toward the crowd. The long, black topcoat hangs on him nearly to his ankles, its length making it appear almost like a cape. Watching Dusty, not anxious at all, an easy expression on his face as people flock to him to say their hellos, instills a tranquil stillness in my body and, finally, I stop fidgeting.

He works the room, hugging women, shaking the hands of men, slapping the backs of croupiers, powwowing with them all, effortlessly slipping from one person to the next, giving everybody just enough face time where they feel valued but not enough where he's keeping himself from somebody else, flashing a smile at just the right time, every time.

His presence tugs on the gravity of the space, has a physical effect on the atmosphere. People who know him drift toward him to get their moment, and those who don't notice his influence unfold on those who do, and view him with intrigue in their eyes.

He mingles for fifteen minutes or so, while I go to the bar for a Pellegrino. When he's done chatting he removes his coat, tucking it under his arm, and scans the apartment, his blue eyes narrow and serious. I can tell he's looking for me.

I take a final swig of my drink and head toward him with my coat, a trip that forces me to contort my torso and limbs into a litany of unnatural positions as I pass through the slim gaps between people.

"Dusty," I call, about five feet from him.

He turns and when he sees it's me his eyes grow big and exuberant. "How you feeling?" he asks, a grin on his face.

"As good as I can be."

"Nothing to worry about. It'll all be over soon. How have things been going so far?"

"I found what I was looking for." I nod toward the library, where Zlata is, and whisper, "Left wall, above the opening into the dining room."

"Well…" He adjusts the knot of his tie and smirks. "That's good." He laughs, slightly, something he couldn't help but do, not due to humor, but delight, the sound bubbling out of his voice box like boiling water from a pot. The fact that I located the camera, the first official completed item of our battle plan, has put the plot in motion, has placed us one step closer to the money.

"When were you thinking of meeting me back at the bar?" I ask. "For that drink we talked about."

He glimpses his watch. "I was going to make that phone call I have to make at one AM. Say one ten?"

"See you then."

He nods, then slips into the crowd, where within five seconds someone recognizes him and yells, "Dusty, you son of a gun, get over here and say hi."

During the next half hour I suck down three more little green bottles of Pellegrino and make two trips to the bathroom. Checking the time on my phone, I see it's 12:57 AM, three minutes before Dusty calls in the police scare.

He's going to sneak off into an empty room in the apartment and from a landline telephone, as opposed to his cell which could be traced back to him, ring the front desk downstairs, say he's an officer from the NYPD, tell the attendant they've been receiving a lot of noise complaints from tenants about a rowdy party in the penthouse, and kindly ask if someone from the building staff could go upstairs to notify the event organizer that the cops are on the way to discuss an acceptable volume.

Finding out a couple NYPD officers are stopping by should prompt Igor to shut the function down, just like he did the last time the police were on their way.

I look at my phone again. 1:00 AM. Go time. I search for Dusty's dirty-blond head among those of the fifty or so guests, spotting it near a craps table. He floats through the medley of attendees and, when his body comes to an angle where his profile is visible, I notice a shadowy line running across his cheek, his jaw clamped, likely from a rush of adrenaline. His face disappears from my view as he turns, then all of him disappears down a hallway.

My right foot taps the marble floor as time passes. *Nud. Nud. Nud.*

Looking past the dizzying action at the gaming tables, I notice him resurface. I try to read his expression, hoping to infer if the call went smoothly. But it's tough to tell. His face hasn't broken from the look it had when I saw him last, his jaw still tight with adrenaline, his eyes still steely.

A woman touches his shoulder and throws her hands up as if to say, *I haven't seen you tonight yet.* He brusquely offers a hello and continues moving.

He leans against the bar, folds his arms, and says to me out of the side of his mouth, "I got through."

"You did?" I ask, a jolt of nervous energy zapping through me.

"Any minute now."

We peer through the scenery ahead, gamblers studying their cards, croupiers spinning roulette wheels, waitresses bustling about with drink trays, at the elevator doors in the foyer. If things go as planned an employee from this building, Tyche Place, should arrive soon for a word with the event organizer.

Watching, waiting, watching, waiting. Nothing. No activity in the foyer except the first guard scratching the side of his face a couple times.

The suspense is palpable inside me, with a temperature and weight and position, hot and heavy and high, a big burning ball in my throat.

Dusty and I don't speak, both of us too focused on the view of the elevator. I can hear the band, now playing "Livin' Thing" by Electric Light Orchestra, however I'm so wrapped up in my sense of vision that my sense of sound feels watered down, the music not seeming like it's coming from this apartment, but one in a neighboring building.

In about three minutes the vertical crease between the elevator doors widens. A man in a burgundy suit steps out. Is he a guest? Does he work for the building? Is he someone else?

The guard greets him. They exchange words, which aren't audible to Dusty and me from back here. As they talk the man slowly pivots his shoulders to face the guard head-on, revealing a small rectangular object glimmering on his chest. A name tag. It must be, which means he must be a building employee.

I nudge Dusty's arm. He's so absorbed by the interaction between the guard and this man that he doesn't even notice. I nudge him again, harder this time. He looks. I point at my chest, signaling about the name tag. Dusty tips me a slight nod of agreement, like he saw it too.

After about thirty seconds of conversing, the guard, with an alertness in his step, stomps down a hallway.

Moisture wraps my skull from my forehead's hairline to the nape of my neck. When he returns, another figure is with him. Igor.

Igor and the man with the name tag dive into a dialogue. A few moments pass. Worry drips into Igor's expression. They shake hands, then the man with the name tag turns and taps the elevator button and gets inside.

Once the doors close Igor clenches the guard's shoulder, pulls the giant man's ear down to his level, and whispers something into it. The guard nods twice.

This is it. Any second and Dusty and I need to spring into action.

A prickly sensation works its way up my body from my feet, stopping at my armpits. It's numbing, everything beneath it, my guts and crotch and legs, without feeling, while everything above it, my shoulders and neck and head, is extra-sensitive. Though I can't feel my right leg, when I look down at it I see it pumping.

Igor marches into the main room. "Everybody, let me have your attention for a moment," he shouts, his voice streaming through the large space. "Stop the bets. Everyone."

The croupiers become still, so do the gamblers. The band awkwardly fades out of the song it's playing, the dozen or so people on the dance floor freezing mid-move.

"I regret this, but we're going to need to conclude the evening early," Igor says. "Please proceed to the door to the stairwell behind me. I'm sorry for the inconvenience. But the night is over. Everyone must leave. Immediately."

A loose marble tile on the floor tremors beneath my foot as the heavy herd of guests moves toward the exit. I put my jacket back on. Dusty does the same, leaving the buttons undone for access to the bag below.

His hands are at his sides and his fingers, partially cloaked by the long sleeves of the one-size-too-big topcoat, wiggle in anticipation. He nods at me as if to ask, *Ready?* and I nod back. He gestures for me to follow him and leads us, on the edge of the crowd, along the wall toward the library where Zlata is, my right shoulder rubbing against the hung velvet blankets as we advance.

A congestion of people is in the hall between the main and cashier rooms, waving their briefcase claim tickets, barking their numbers at Zlata. Behind the arms flailing through the air, I notice Boris the guard open the safe. Another guard scurries to his side with two black garbage bags and the men hurry to transfer the money inside.

Not far from them are the chips, that glorious smorgasbord of color. Just as we foresaw, nobody is paying them any attention amid the chaos. The guards are fitted with the pressing task of hiding the house cash. The gamblers are focused on their briefcases of money. And Zlata is fixated on retrieving them. At this unique moment, nobody gives a shit about chips.

Except Dusty and me.

Dusty assesses the scene for a few seconds and says, "I'm getting in there from the side. From the dining room. You push your way far enough to the front of that line where you have an angle. I'll be waiting under the archway. Give me a thumbs-up when you're ready."

"Okay," I say, my voice wispy with bated breath.

He lets out a potent exhale and jumps up and down a couple times, like boxers do in their corners moments before the opening bell. He slaps me on the shoulder and makes for the dining room, his long jacket flapping behind him.

I turn to the cashier area, about twenty-five guests crammed between it and me in the hallway. "Number seventeen," a voice shouts at Zlata.

"Twelve goddammit," another yells.

My head down, my elbows tucked against my ribs, I grind my way through the tightness toward the front.

"I'm next," a voice whines to Zlata. "Number twenty-nine."

"*I* was next," another fires back.

I keep moving, slower now, an obstruction of suit jackets in front of me, blacks and blues and grays. I can see into the library but just barely, slices of it visible between the bodies. The guards, with stuffed bags of cash slung over their shoulders, lurch through the archway, leaving the empty safe behind. They cut across the dining room toward the stairwell, passing Dusty who lingers near the half-eaten platter of meat medallions.

Within the next minute I move forward about a foot. Shining the laser pointer this far back is bound to snag someone's attention. I need to sneak closer.

"Did anybody see a phone?" I ask the group, then go down to my knees and pretend I'm searching for a dropped one. A few people step aside, clearing a small space for my sham search. I run my palms against the marble like I'm feeling for something. This is working, surprisingly. On all fours I cover more floor than I did on my feet.

I crawl past five different pairs of men's shoes and one set of high heels. A guy in wingtips steps on my right hand, the nail of my ring finger crunching between his sole and the marble. "Ahh, fuck," I grumble as the pain shoots through my knuckles, my wrist, my forearm, my bicep, and my shoulder, not stopping until it hits my collarbone. Fighting through the discomfort, I keep crawling, trying not to contact the floor with my throbbing right ring finger and its reddish-purple nail, instead navigating with the flesh at the base of my thumb.

When I look up I see I'm only three feet or so from the library. In the background, through the arched passage into the dining room, waits Dusty, his face alive with eagerness.

I move another eighteen inches and jut my left arm between the legs of the man in front of me, who's so angry about his still-stowed briefcase he doesn't even notice, and wiggle my hand, a signal to Dusty. His eyes stop on me. I put my right hand, which is still pulsating, into my pocket, groping for the laser pointer.

Soon I feel the grooves of its metal grip on my fingertips. I glance up, making sure nobody at the front of the line is watching Dusty or me. They're not, everybody still concentrated on the briefcases. Assessing the angle of the camera lens, I'm confident my body is out of its eye's view. I aim the laser pointer at it and click the button, a red dot appearing on the wall six inches to the right of the lens. I adjust my beam so it's in the center of the glass.

Then I give Dusty a thumbs-up.

He stares into the library, toward the far wall, watching Zlata, waiting for the perfect moment.

She takes a claim ticket from a man, turns her back to the chips, and walks toward the briefcases. Dusty swoops in, positions himself at the corner of the desk, and parts his jacket with his left hand. My heart thuds hard and heavy, like a stone wrapped in veins and tendons, as I watch his right arm whip over the rack of chips, his elbow pivoting and swinging.

A second passes. I glimpse the crowd. Three seconds. I glance at Dusty. Four seconds. Zlata scans the labels on the cases. Dusty's elbow keeps its flow. Zlata is still searching the labels. Dusty cleans out five columns of gold chips, a hundred-K worth, our goal.

But he doesn't leave.

He bends down and situates himself under the desk. Two more seconds go by. What the hell is he doing? He crouches beside a spare rack of chips still with its lid on.

This lunatic is going for even more.

This wasn't part of the plan.

He peeks at Zlata, then the gamblers, then begins unsnapping the four clamps on the lid. My stone of a heart grows to boulder proportions.

Zlata finds the right briefcase and grabs it. Dusty slides off the lid and starts snagging another gold column from the spare tray. Zlata pulls out the briefcase. Dusty keeps his motion, moving on to a second column. Zlata begins spinning back toward the crowd.

I check the desk. Dusty's gone, the bottom of the top-coat billowing through the archway into the dining room, then out of sight. I remove my finger from the laser-pointer button. Zlata returns her gaze to the crowd.

My mind is overloaded by a singular thought, *Holy shit, I think that just worked.*

I stuff the laser pointer in my pocket, stand, and start traversing the hallway toward the main room. I wind my way into the foyer where I spot Dusty, his jacket now buttoned, on the line of guests filing through the exit.

One of the security guards, holding the door to the stairwell open, shouts, "Let's go. Move. Now." Dusty's arms are crossed over his chest and his face is crowded with nerves.

Something is wrong.

He gazes over his shoulder, I assume to locate me. I wave. He nods toward a close-by bathroom door.

I guess he wants me to go in, so I do. I'm alone in the shadowy bathroom for a bit before he scuttles inside. He closes the door, the only light in the room a low line horizontally flowing below the door slab, providing just enough visibility where we can see each other's shape. He carefully opens his jacket, revealing the burlap bag brimming with the extra chips he chose to snatch.

"Jesus," I say. "That wasn't part of the plan. Are you crazy, you—"

"Screw the plan. We have more money now than we would've with the plan." He grips a handful of chips from atop the heap and passes them to me. "Put these in your pockets. I can't fit them in the bag." I do. Then he hands me another handful. "These too." I squeeze them into my coat, which is now beginning to swell and could seem suspicious.

He attempts to give me a third batch but I tell him, "I can't fit more."

"I think I can manage." He jams the remaining chips in with the rest in his sack.

"You sure?" I ask. "Let's just leave a few behind. Put them under the sink. We have enough. We have a ton." The rumble of footsteps from the gamblers roars outside.

"I got it," he says. "I'll go out first. So nothing looks sketchy, count to ten then come out after." He buttons up his coat, flashes me a grin, barely detectable in the dark, and leaves.

My heart cracks against my chest as my mind counts. Seven. Eight. Nine. Ten.

I step out. I spot Dusty ahead, a few bodies from the exit. We all move forward. Some more. And some more. I glimpse my bulging pockets. I stick my fists in them, trying to give the impression my hands are causing the expansion.

A few people pass through the exit doorway. Dusty gets closer. A few more. A voice yells out from the herd, "Would you quit pushing me?" I see a man in a blue suit squaring up to a man in a black one, angry expressions on their faces.

"I'm just trying to get out of here," the guy in black says.

"Can you do it without knocking me in the back every five seconds?" People stare.

"Get off your high horse."

"Fuck you," the man in blue barks, shoving the other. A punch is thrown. Then another. And another.

The one in black tackles the one in blue. They roll, taking out the legs of a third man, directly in front of Dusty. The third, well over two hundred pounds, falls backwards, coming down on Dusty's right shoulder just before he gets out of the way, knocking him off balance. Dusty struggles to find his footing, his heels smacking against the marble floor. He topples. The other man lands on top of him.

Boris the security guard pounces on the fighting duo, yanking their bodies apart. "Knock it off," he screams. Once he separates them he shifts his attention to Dusty and the third man, both picking themselves up from the floor. Boris's mouth tightens. His complexion reddens.

Scattered by Dusty's feet, next to his dropped cell phone, are a dozen gold chips. Boris's gaze locks on them.

As Dusty stands, a couple more fall out of his jacket. Boris hollers something in Russian, heaves a woman out of his way, and hightails toward Dusty, everyone in the foyer freezing, viewing.

Dusty scoots through the stairwell doorway, out of sight. "Dusty," I shout, shouldering my way through the guests, trailing him and Boris onto the steps.

I can't see them, a couple stories below me, but I can hear them, the bang of their shoes on the metal stairs, the occasional Russian curse word. I wind down the levels, knocking into bodies every few feet. Floor 18. Floor 17. Floor 16.

Looking below, I can see the top of Dusty's head as he turns a corner. Soon I spot Boris curving around the same one. I go faster. My lungs heat up. Floor 9. Floor 8. Floor 7. I peek beneath me, Dusty close to ground level, Boris a flight behind.

I push myself harder, trying to catch up. Glancing down, I no longer see them, both must have made it to the lobby. Floor 3. Floor 2. I'm panting. Lobby. I swing open the door, feeling the intense heat from the ceiling vents. No sign of them. The attendant at the front desk has an overwhelmed expression. I scurry across the blue rug with the "T" on it and blast out the front door into the blizzard.

No indication of Dusty or Boris. The storm has worsened, no cars on the road, no people on the sidewalk except for ten or so event guests waiting for rides. I look left, then right, only to see the dim faces of closed businesses, the white of the snowflakes washing over the shadow-blackened walls, light and dark combining to create a grayness that encapsulates the entire block.

A noise rings out. Quick, metallic. Fright fills the faces of the event guests outside Tyche Place. They retreat inside.

What was that noise?

I turn the corner of the building, heading toward the sound's origin. I notice a small gleam of color mixed in with the sprawling grayness. Gold. Getting closer, I see it's a chip from upstairs. A thousand dollars, down in front of me, yet I don't think to pick it up, my mind only focused on finding Dusty.

Another gold chip is up the road. Then another. Dusty must be leaking them as he runs. My eyes follow their path, and in the distance, hazy through the blizzard, are two bodies, Dusty's sprinting and Boris's extending a pistol close behind.

The noise rings out again. These are gunshots.

"Nooo," I shout, stomping through the snow toward them. I don't know how I'd help if I caught up, but still I'm compelled to go.

The sound of a third gunshot violently pierces the stormy quiet. Dusty limps for two strides, then falls.

He's hit.

"Dusty," I yell, still over a block away.

I notice movement. Wearily he stands, unbuttoning his jacket. Then throws it in the air, the gold chips still inside the burlap bag spurting all over like firework sparks.

Boris, about to discharge another shot at Dusty to finish him off, lowers the weapon and hustles to collect the discarded chips, recovering the cash they represent more important to him than ridding their thief of his life. A crafty move by Dusty.

However, Dusty is far from okay. As Boris collects the chips, Dusty, clutching his right thigh, limps toward an alley, blood oozing from it on the virgin snow behind him.

"Dusty, wait," I yell. However, I don't even think he hears me.

He slips into the alley. By the time I get up there and gaze into it, I see no sign of him. The line of blood on the white ground ends, and all that's before me is an endless amount of gray.

Sixteen

I don't know where I am.

I've just been walking, deeper into the folds of a storm enfolding me with mere feet of visibility and then a flickering, nameless gray, like static on a television set.

My mind is broken. My thoughts are nothing more than bits of awareness, whipping around without order inside my head, just like the snowflakes outside it.

Dusty is dead.

Or will be soon.

His phone dropped from his pocket when he fell down at the event. He had no way of contacting me or anyone else for help. Adrift on these ghostly streets, spewing blood from his leg, he likely passed out, rendering himself a fatal victim, or soon to be one, of the icy elements.

I need to get out of the cold. Dusty is dead. I don't remember where my limo is parked. Dusty is dead. I can't feel my face. Dusty is dead. The laser pointer. Dusty is dead. The two men fighting by the stairwell door. Dusty is dead. The third man tumbling. Dusty is dead. The chips on the marble floor. Dusty is dead. Boris's dark eyes. Dusty is dead. I don't know where I am. Dusty is dead.

Within my brain's anarchy, some thought particle stabilizes for a second. And it tells me where to go.

The visibility is so terrible I can't read the street sign ahead until I'm two feet away. 7th and West 14th.

My thigh muscles battle the head-on wind as I advance through New York. The ice storm masks the scenery I'm used to on the sides of these roads, the banners and benches and billboards and bodies and buildings. The whole of modern society is hidden. I feel like a caveman on a quest across Tundra, nothing among me but nature, no external instructions about what to do, my only compass my internal voice.

An hour and a half later I make it to my destination. My freezing body is shriveled inside my soaked jacket, my frame mostly rattling bone. I enter the code on the intercom to buzz unit 3G. Beeps chirp from the speaker. Then stop. No answer.

I call 3G again. Again, no answer. A third time. The beeps kick in, then quiet, giving way to, "Hello," a groggy quality to it, a product of a voice just asleep.

"Hi," I say.

"Who is this?"

"It's me."

Three seconds pass. "Brian?"

"I need...I need to...something bad happened." Silence.

"Do you know what time it is?"

"Something bad happened. Really bad. Really fucking bad."

"What do you *need*?" Samantha asks, ticked off.

I don't know how to reply. I answer as honestly as I can, "I just need to see you right now."

"I have to go to bed. And you're a liar. I don't know who you are."

I place my face closer to the intercom, closer to her voice, closer to her. "My best friend is dead." Heat builds beneath my clenched eyelids, the only bits of warmth on my body.

The fuzzy hum from the speaker stops. The connection cuts. She's gone, hung up. I inch my face closer to the intercom. Closer even, my cheek now against the frostbitten metal.

Ten seconds go by. A ring radiates into my ear. A bolt clacks. The door unlocks. I turn to it, the soft light of the dorm's foyer glowing within the glass panes. I grip the handle and step into the warmth of the building.

A few moments later I'm standing in front of familiar door 3G. It opens, revealing Samantha in pajamas and a ponytail. Her eyes survey my broken-down appearance, her nurturing instincts surfacing, her expression stirring with concern. She motions me into her room. I enter.

The only light is from the lamp on her night table, bright on her sheets, then dimming as it diffuses across the room, settling faintly on her dorm mate's empty bed in the opposite corner. I catch my reflection in the full-length mirror propped against the wall. My cheeks are a mess, a layer of skin churned off by the hail. I imagine these pieces of me, this topmost layer of my face, mixed in with everything else blowing around in the storm.

I sit on Samantha's bed, a circle of dampness swelling on her sheets from my wet clothing.

"Someone *died*?" she asks, watching me with her lower teeth pinned against her upper lip and her hand placed over her heart, a posture that's both suspicious and sympathetic, unsure about my unexpected arrival while sorry about my dejected appearance and whatever must've caused it. "Tell me what happened, Brian."

Reflexively, I start probing my mind for a lie, a dance around the truth of what really went on tonight, around my double life.

But I don't go through with it.

Something in me snuffs this voice. A new voice begins building inside me, from a different place than the untruthful one, a spot in the pit of my soul, a river wrapped in a forest of my darkest fears and insecurities. A dam across the river breaks from its power and the water rushes through, flowing around the ugly trees, up into my mouth, and out of it as honesty. "For the last few weeks," I tell Samantha, "I've been driving a limo for an underground gambling circle run by the Russian mob."

And from there the truth keeps gushing out of me. I tell her about my brother and his drug debt, about the need for quick cash, about my father the cop and protecting him from everything, about the thousand bucks a night I earned from the casino, about my boss Igor, about how scared I was of him, about how terrible I felt when he hit her, about the plan to get him back, about the robbery earlier tonight, about how

I did it for her, about the security guard, about the gunshots, about the death of my best friend.

By the time I'm done the dampness from my clothing grows to a ring over nearly half the bed. Samantha, her eyes motionless yet loaded with emotion, stares at me from just outside the beam of the night-table lamp. A half-minute goes by.

Then she sits beside me, her pajama bottoms settling onto the wet sheets. A tear trickles from her pear-colored eye. She dabs it with her thumb, descends her hand to my palm, and nestles her fingers between mine.

Seventeen

Dusty never returned to his cabin.

It's been a little over a month. For the first week I continued living there, waiting, day after day and night after night, for him to show up. And he never did. Though he lost his phone the evening of the robbery, I figured if he were alive he would've gotten a new one. I tried his number at least ten times a day, hoping he'd answer. And he never did. The calls would go right to voicemail, until one day that even stopped. And his brief greeting, the only trace of him I had left, "Hey, it's Dusty, leave a message," was taken from me too.

I quit driving for the gambling events which, as hoped, tanked in popularity after the havoc we caused. The last I heard attendance is down to a couple dozen. I even quit Big Hitter entirely. Once I did my father agreed to take me back into the house, however, our relationship is far from mended. I have a long way to go to earn back his trust.

His trust, however, is still something my brother has. The morning after the robbery, after I emptied my pockets, twenty-two gold chips stared back at me, which I'd forgotten Dusty even gave me, in the bathroom during one of the last moments of his life.

Twenty-two thousand dollars. As promised, Vince bought them. As promised, I saved Kip from his debt. And my dad gladly knows nothing of it.

A few thousand bucks were left over, which I've been living off of in lieu of my Big Hitter salary. I'll get a new job soon. However, I have a lot of thinking to do before choosing a path. Thinking, as Dusty used to say, "really thinking," is scary and hard. But it's the only way to circumvent convention, and live the life you want versus the one society tells you to want.

I walk into the kitchen and open the refrigerator, readying myself to make a turkey sandwich, a daily, noon tradition since I've been unemployed.

"You got some mail," my mom says, floating into the kitchen from the den to refill her coffee mug.

"All right," I say, pulling the cold cuts from the meat compartment.

I set some on a slice of semolina bread, top them with lettuce and tomatoes, then squirt Dijon mustard on another slice and squish everything together. I grab a can of Coke and sit at the kitchen counter. As I take my first bite, I eye the messy stack of mail nearby.

Sifting through it, I pluck out anything with my name on it. A credit-card advertisement. An update from my college's alumni association. A form for a magazine-package subscription.

One envelope stands out. The writing on it isn't in English. No return address. With a closer inspection of the stamp and markings, I notice it's from Brazil. I open it. All that's inside is a photo. Of a wooden chair, on display at some street fair with a for-sale tag on it in a foreign language. I don't recognize any of the faces in the photo, all seeming to be random bystanders' at the fair.

Puzzled, I flip the picture over in search of more information. And what I find stuns me. A hand-scribbled note that says, "I might not have enough money to do Europe yet, but South America ain't a bad place to start."

Nobody signed it. But I know who wrote it.

Dusty.

He's alive.

My mind spins, in a jubilant way. I look at the photo again. That's one of Dusty's chairs. And it's magnificent to know that not only is he alive, but living his dream. Traveling the world, woodworking.

Half the money I pocketed is his. And I want to give it to him. But on his note he doesn't even ask. He doesn't even provide contact information.

I reason I can just give it to him when I see him in New York. However, it dawns on me that he can't come back to New York. At least not now. Not with the Russian mob ready to kill him for thievery. And if he eventually does, it'll likely be with a low profile, or even a new profile with a totally different name.

And as I think of this, the jubilation that's been coursing through me slows down. And it comes to a stop when I realize there's a very good possibility, though alive, I'll never see Dusty Walnen again.

However, I'm soon able to make peace with this. Just knowing he's out there, living the life he wants, will be a constant reminder that I must do the same.

Footsteps fill the kitchen. Kip, a backpack hanging off him, grabs his keys off the counter, ready to go to class. He notices me staring down at the photo. Curious, he steps to my side and has a look.

"What the hell is that? A chair?"

"Yep. A really quality one."

He studies the picture for a few seconds. "It just seems like any old chair."

"No it doesn't," I say. "It has that *exact* right look."

About

Lion on Fire is a book by Ted Galdi. He's also the author of the novels *Elixir* and *An American Cage*, and the short story *A Road to Nowhere*. To take advantage of his free offers, visit his website at tedgaldi.com.